Chelsea fro
an expressi

The sound of Raf's deep voice drained all the color from her face. A hundred conflicting thoughts fought for supremacy as she battled to retain a semblance of calm. Then she slowly turned to face him.

He appeared taller than she remembered, she noticed dimly. His broad frame was sheathed in expensive suiting, and his features were every bit as forceful as they had ever been.

Rafael Hamilton. Son of a Texas oil millionaire whose wife held legitimate claim to an honored branch of the Spanish nobility.

A man who was many things—financial entrepreneur, undisputed head of Houghton-Hamilton. He was also her husband.

HELEN BIANCHIN, originally from New Zealand, met the man she would marry on a tobacco farm in Australia. Danilo, an Italian immigrant, spoke little English. Helen's Italian was nil. But communicate they did, and within eight weeks Danilo found the words to ask Helen to marry him. With such romantic beginnings, it's a wonder that the author waited until after the birth of their third child to begin her prolific romance-writing career.

Books by Helen Bianchin

HARLEQUIN PRESENTS

271—VINES OF SPLENDOUR
289—STORMY POSSESSION
409—DEVIL IN COMMAND
415—EDGE OF SPRING
457—THE SAVAGE TOUCH
527—WILDFIRE ENCOUNTER
695—YESTERDAY'S SHADOW
720—SAVAGE PAGAN
744—SWEET TEMPEST
751—DARK TYRANT
839—BITTER ENCORE
975—DARK ENCHANTMENT
1111—AN AWAKENING DESIRE

HARLEQUIN ROMANCE

2010—BEWILDERED HAVEN
2084—AVENGING ANGEL
2175—THE HILLS OF HOME
2387—MASTER OF ULURU

Don't miss any of our special offers. Write to us at the following address for information on our newest releases.

Harlequin Reader Service
901 Fuhrmann Blvd., P.O. Box 1397, Buffalo, NY 14240
Canadian address: P.O. Box 603,
Fort Erie, Ont. L2A 5X3

HELEN BIANCHIN

touch the flame

Harlequin Books

TORONTO • NEW YORK • LONDON
AMSTERDAM • PARIS • SYDNEY • HAMBURG
STOCKHOLM • ATHENS • TOKYO • MILAN

Harlequin Presents first edition February 1990
ISBN 0-373-11240-8

Original hardcover edition published in 1989
by Mills & Boon Limited

Printed in U.S.A.

CHAPTER ONE

CHELSEA slid in behind the wheel of her silver Porsche, fired the engine, then eased the powerful sports car down the driveway towards ornately scrolled iron gates guarding the entrance to the elegant-storeyed Tudor-style home she occupied in the exclusive Sydney suburb of Castlecrag.

A home, she mused idly as she activated the remote-control unit to allow her exit, that was much too large for one person. It would be infinitely more practical if she opted for a stylish apartment in any one of the number of expensive high-rise buildings that dotted the foreshore of the inner city. Except that every time she gave the idea serious thought, there was an intrinsic pull to negate it.

Besides, she wasn't alone. Hannah and Will Somerfield looked after the house and grounds, tending both with loving care, and there was a small menagerie of animals. Two darling shih-tzu dogs, an Alsatian of doubtful breeding who displayed the quintessence of affection to those of whom he approved, but who became totally ferocious with itinerant strangers, a Himalayan Persian cat with an impeccable background and papers to prove it, and a pink-plumed galah parrot who whiled away his captive hours in one of the most well-equipped aviaries in southern Australasia; not one of whom she could bear to part with.

The gates closed behind her, their faint, well-oiled clunk sounding simultaneously with the refined purr from the engine as she headed the car down the tree-studded avenue that connected with an expressway leading into the city.

It was a glorious morning, the sky a clear, brilliant blue, cloudless apart from a fairy-floss drift of delicate cirrus-like cloud, and the sun's warmth already held promise of sweltering summer heat mixed with high humidity.

She should have made an earlier start, Chelsea reflected with wry resignation a short while later as she eased the Porsche to a snail-like pace in heavy city-bound traffic. At this rate it would be another twenty minutes before she reached the office building in which she worked.

Impatience would do no good at all. Perhaps if she hadn't stayed out so late, and the hours between two and seven had been spent sleeping instead of restlessly tossing and turning, she wouldn't now feel tired and more than a little jaded.

Without conscious thought, she slid a tape into the cassette recorder, and within seconds the soothing voice of Lionel Richie filtered through the speakers, blocking out all other intrusive sound.

Listening to the velvet-smooth tones of the popular singer stirred to life a disturbing memory, one she'd fought hard to ignore for more than two years. And been relatively successful, she thought with a touch of self-mockery, until recently.

Perhaps it was the festive season which was to blame—Christmas trees and carols, anticipation and joy, gifts and giving.

Maybe if . . . A faint sigh whispered from Chelsea's lips. There were too many *ifs* for it ever to have worked. Her father's unsuccessful battle with cancer necessitating her return to Australia from the States two years ago could not be blamed, nor could——

A harsh horn-blast penetrated the interior of the car, and with a faint flush she shifted gear and sent the Porsche moving, glad that she couldn't hear what the motorist behind her had angrily mouthed in her direction.

Damn! It didn't pay to indulge in senseless reverie while driving, she thought with a self-deprecatory grimace. Especially in the midst of peak hour city traffic.

At last the tall concrete edifice housing her workplace loomed into sight and, depressing the indicator, Chelsea swung in behind a queue of vehicles heading down into the underground car park.

The elevator was almost filled to capacity, and she nodded to a colleague, a pleasant smile fixed in place as she stood silent; a slim, elegantly dressed young woman who bore the unmistakable air of inbred sophistication. Her make-up was understated, but cleverly effective, highlighting flawless skin, wide-spaced green eyes and a generous mouth. Ash-blonde hair fell to her shoulders, its thick, tapering length brushed into a simple style that made her look much younger than her twenty-five years.

The elevator paused several times before Chelsea was able to alight at the thirty-first level, where she moved swiftly across the marble-tiled lobby, past reception, the executive lounge, to the suite she shared with her secretary in the sought-after south-eastern corner of the building.

From this height, the view through tinted plate glass was nothing short of spectacular in every direction: the sparkling waters of Port Jackson with its plethora of moving sea-craft, the unique architecture of the Opera House vying for supremacy with the steel expanse of the famed Harbour Bridge.

Usually Chelsea delighted in the panoramic vista, but this morning she crossed to her desk, opened her briefcase, removed a sheaf of papers, then depressed the intercom switch.

'Susan, bring me the file on Hamilton Holdings.' Chelsea paused fractionally, and made a concentrated effort to dispel the faint weariness that had settled behind her eyes and held promise of burgeoning into a full-blown headache. 'And coffee, please. Black, strong, with two sugars. Jonathan Prendergaast is very insistent I see him at eleven this morning.'

She released the intercom switch and ran a swift red-lacquered fingernail down the list of appointments pencilled in her diary for the day. One, possibly two, could be postponed until tomorrow. She tapped the book absently, a faint frown creasing her brow.

As an accountant, Jonathan was both skilled and highly qualified, his promotion into the firm coinciding with the amalgamation of Houghton-Hamilton. The reason for his telephone call just prior to her leaving home this morning was unprecedented and therefore perplexing, she decided pensively as she glanced round the room.

The office bore all the trappings of success, she thought idly. The furnishings were selected to impress, their designer elegance a signature of refined simplicity.

The vague ache behind her eyes began to intensify, and combined with a feeling of general lassitude that surely had to be related to a series of pre-Christmas drinks and social functions that were a pre-requisite in the run-down to the year's end.

A discreet tap on the outer door preceded Susan's entrance into the room, and Chelsea proffered the slim brunette a grateful smile.

'Thanks, Susan.' She took the coffee from her secretary's hand and set it on the desk. The aromatic steam activated the digestive juices inside her stomach, making her increasingly aware that she'd overslept and skipped breakfast.

'Would you contact Rosemount and Jenkins, and diplomatically reshuffle their appointments to this afternoon?' She lifted the cup to her lips and took an appreciative sip, reflecting that if this morning's meeting with Jonathan dragged on she'd probably miss out on lunch as well.

'Of course. I'll attend to it immediately,' Susan responded briskly. For a moment she let the mask of alert efficiency slip as her clear blue eyes clouded with concern. 'You look pale. Are you feeling all right?'

'Tired,' Chelsea admitted with the semblance of a smile. 'Animated social chit-chat combined with lack of oxygen and too much cigarette smoke isn't my idea of a fun evening.' Her expression assumed unaccustomed cynicism. 'And I'm prepared to go on oath that someone spiked the fruit punch.'

'Doubtless you dined on caviare, crackers, and assorted gourmet nibbles.'

'Dare I confess?' she owned ruefully, aware that Susan, her senior by some fifteen years, had faithfully paid her dues at Houghton-Hamilton, rising from the typing pool to become Sam Houghton's secretary in the days when there was no Hamilton tagged on to Houghton and Chelsea was a leggy schoolgirl.

'I'll send out for sandwiches,' Susan declared firmly, 'which you will eat before attending the meeting. Fainting on the job is hardly in keeping with your image.'

'True,' Chelesa agreed drily, only too aware how difficult it had been to assume partial control of a financial empire which had links extending to every major capital in the world. Several sceptics had seen her decision to take up a seat on the board of directors after her father's death as a frivolous whim by an attractive young woman with a degree in business management, no practical experience and absolutely no necessity to gain any. Except a personal need to prove herself. At the time it had provided a legitimate and logical reason for her to remain in Sydney. It also gave her an 'out' on a personal relationship that had begun on shaky ground and rapidly deteriorated into a state of unenviable non-existence.

Chelsea glanced pensively at the ivory manila folder resting on her desk, then slid it forward and flipped open the cover. As a résumé, it was impressive, with cross-references to every acquisition since the incorporation of both companies; an amalgamation which three years ago had caused a considerable stir in the business sector. Hamilton had its roots in the States, an established firm which had plodded a path of mediocrity for years until the eldest son of the foundation member had taken over the reins and brought Hamiltion into the forefront, gaining well-earned kudos among a number of peers who had reluctantly made room in their upper echelons for a man whose very name had soon become synonymous with tenacity and power.

Property, shares; an enviable and streamlined composite of blue-chip investment with some calculated 'wildcat' ventures. Most had escalated more than favourably to show excellent returns, while others had been sold off before they could establish a loss.

A very shrewd portfolio, Chelsea determined idly as she ran a practised eye over the latest gains. Although one appeared a sleeper, and she made a mental note to query its purchase at the meeting, which, she noted with a quick glance at her watch, was due to begin in thirty minutes.

A slight frown furrowed her brow. Consultations with Jonathan were an integral part of business and essential to ensure maximum efficiency, but the reason for today's last-minute scheduling eluded her. For some unknown reason she felt vaguely uneasy, almost as if some sixth sense was attempting to give an advance warning.

As her secretary came back into the room, Chelsea's mouth widened into an appreciative smile.

'Whatever would I do without you?' she smiled

as Susan placed a tray down on to the desk, dispensed steaming liquid into a fresh cup and set about removing plastic cling-wrap from a plate of delectable-looking, wafer-thin sandwiches.

'Manage admirably, I imagine,' Susan responded with an irrepressible grin.

Chelsea wrinkled her nose slightly, and her green eyes assumed a humorous sparkle. 'Behind every successful executive is an efficient secretary. You're one of the best.'

'Ah—a compliment!'

'Sincerely meant, I assure you.'

Susan's expression softened. 'I know. Thank you.' She became a model of brisk competence. 'Now eat, please.'

'Yes, ma'am.' Chelsea reached out and selected a salmon and lettuce-filled triangle, then followed it with another. It surprised her to discover just how hungry she was, and after a second cup of coffee she felt a surge of renewed energy, sufficient to dictate instructions regarding data she required and the calls she wanted to make prior to midday. *If* the meeting didn't drag on too long.

Without further thought she extracted a make-up pouch from her bag and crossed to the small alcove adjacent to her office. Touching up her mouth with lipstick, she added a clear gloss, then smoothed her hair before giving her watch a final glance. Two minutes to eleven. Punctuality was something she aimed for at all times, forming part of a careful strategy she'd painstakingly created.

The boardroom was situated opposite her office, and she walked into the large room to find only one occupant seated at the long mahogany table.

'Good morning,' Chelsea greeted him as she took the chair Jonathan Prendergaast held out for her. 'Thank you,' she murmured, her expression composed as she waited until he was seated before meeting his enigmatic gaze.

'Calling this meeting was your idea,' she began smoothly. 'Perhaps you'd care to elaborate?'

He shifted in his chair, easing his lanky frame into a more comfortable position as he picked up a pen and tapped it absently against the folder lying in front of him. 'Certain rumours have begun to circulate of which I think you should be aware.'

'What rumours?' She schooled her features to remain bland, although there was a strange prickling sensation at her nape.

'In connection with a proposed takeover.'

'Of Houghton-Hamilton? Don't be absurd!' she countered with conviction. 'If it was true, I would be one of the first to hear.'

He considered her carefuly for several seconds. 'Not if the rumour originated in America.'

Something clenched inside Chelsea's stomach, and she steeled herself to respond with cool deliberation. 'I trust you've attempted to confirm this with Raf?'

'Of course.'

Yes, she breathed wearily. Jonathan Prendergaast maintained weekly contact with Raf Hamilton —wherever the dynamic head of Houghton-Hamilton happened to be in the world. His residences alone numbered three in the States, from a condominium in Florida to a palatial home in Los Angeles. In New York his apartment was high on Fifth Avenue with a fantastic view over Central Park. Then there was a terraced flat in London's fashionable Docklands. He travelled so extensively, he commanded his own private jet.

'He denied the rumours?' Chelsea voice was controlled but she felt as if her features had assumed a mask-like expression. Suddenly she was aware of her own vulnerability, as well as being the focus of a pair of observant, all-assessing eyes.

'He would only confirm that he had knowledge of them.'

Chelsea managed to meet his concerted gaze unblinkingly, aware just how much effort it cost to present a calm, unruffled façade.

'I see.' She leaned back in her chair as she marshalled her thoughts. 'One assumes he intends to inform us if they hold any substance? And what steps he intends to take?'

'Of course,' Jonathan agreed. 'In the meantime, he insists the information be regarded with the strictest confidence.'

'In that case, we can do little else but await further news.'

The accountant inclined his head in silent acquiescence, and she looked at him with careful circumspection, aware of the possibility that he might be deliberately withholding information. It was no secret that Jonathan Prendergaast was Raf Hamilton's right-hand man, despite *her* position. A fact she had learnt to cope with and accept.

'That's it?' Chelsea queried, wanting the meeting to end. Jonathan's character was too close to that of his American-based employer; even the man's height and dark good looks held a clone-like resemblance. It was something she found vaguely disturbing whenever they were alone together, despite their relationship never intruding beyond a strictly professional level.

'Not quite.'

'You mean there's more?' If she took notice of her immediate instinct, she could almost imagine he was stalling.

'I'd like access to the file on Hamilton Holdings. When you've finished with it, of course?'

'I'll leave it with Susan,' Chelsea concurred. 'Will midday suit? I have a few more items I'd like to check.'

'This afternoon will be fine.'

She stood to her feet, aware of a need to be in control and not merely a participant in a game involving power-play. 'Thank you, Jonathan, for ensuring that I heard the rumour first-hand.' She could afford to be generous. Technically, by virtue of her inheritance, she held a thirty-five-per-cent stake in Hamilton-Houghton.

'How professionally diplomatic!' a deep voice drawled from behind her.

Chelsea froze, her features momentarily locked into an expressionless mask as she felt the colour drain from her face. A hundred conflicting thoughts fought for supremacy as she battled to retain a semblance of calm, aware that every second she remained immobile amounted to a victory against her.

Assembling a polite façade took tremendous effort, but she managed it, and her movements were mechanically automatic as she slowly turned to face her aggressor, her eyes dilating slightly as the visual image of the man she'd endeavoured to push to the back of her mind manifested itself into reality.

He appeared taller than she remembered, she registered dimly; his broad frame was sheathed in expensive suiting, and his features were every bit as forceful as they had ever been.

Rafael Hamilton. Son of a Texan oil multi-millionaire whose wife held legitimate claim to an honoured branch of the Spanish nobility.

A man who was many things—financial entrepreneur, undisputed head of Houghton-Hamilton. He was also her husband.

CHAPTER TWO

'HELLO, Raf.' Chelsea sounded quietly composed, when inside she was a mass of nerves, each separate fibre tautening to its farthest limitation. She'd lived this moment a thousand times over the past two years, aware that it was only a matter of time before Raf instigated a confrontation. The only question in her mind had been where and when.

'Chelsea.' His voice held infinite mockery beneath a veneer of politeness and she forced herself to hold his gaze, refusing to quake under the ruthless intensity of his deliberate appraisal.

As an attempt to undermine her confidence, it almost succeeded. Three years ago she had succumbed to his brand of dynamic power and opted for the line of least resistance. Now her eyes deepened until they resembled cyan-blue pools of obsidian ice as she adopted an inwardly defensive stance.

'If you'll excuse me?' Jonathan said smoothly, moving away from the table. 'I'll be in my office.'

Chelsea afforded the accountant a brief glance, accompanied by an even briefer dismissive nod, before returning her attention to the man standing less than three feet distant.

'You could have let me know of your impending visit,' she declared with scant attempt at civility.

One eyebrow lifted in a silent gesture of wry cynicism. 'Given you advance warning, so to speak?' His lips twisted into a humourless smile. 'I informed Jonathan.'

'Of course.' It was impossible to keep the sarcastic edge from her voice.

'And chose to see you alone,' Raf added hardily.

Her chin lifted fractionally. 'For which I should be grateful, I assume?'

His gaze became hooded. 'Would you have preferred me to walk into your office unannounced?'

'I'm sure I could have handled it,' she responded coolly, refusing to allow his presence to prove a threat to her equilibrium.

Raf's smile was a mirthless facsimile. 'Perhaps you could, at that.'

Chelsea longed to fling angrily that she'd grown up a lot since the days when she had lived with him as his wife. But she refrained, aware that he would judge the uttering of such an avowal as an attempt at self-conviction, rather than fact.

'Shall we dispense with the inanities and move straight to the reason for your surprise visit?' She felt in control, although distinctly wary. Conducting any form of verbal intercourse with Raf usually disintegrated into a play of words from which he invariably emerged the victor. 'You must want something. You wouldn't be here if you didn't.'

'Astute,' he drawled, his eyes alert with a compelling intensity. And, unless she was mistaken, cynical amusement.

His height was intimidating, and she made a perfunctory gesture towards a nearby chair. 'Why not sit down?' She'd feel more in control if he wasn't looming over her.

'Alternatively, we could combine this with an early lunch.' He lifted his shoulders in a careless shrug. 'I haven't eaten in several hours.'

Lunch? Chelsea viewed him cautiously. She'd far prefer to keep whatever they had to say to each other on a strictly business footing. Sharing a meal in the intimacy of a restaurant wasn't conducive to formality.

'Surely you aren't afraid?'

She almost resorted to the type of retaliatory remark he sought to evoke, and her eyes flashed, silently warring with his steely grey gaze. 'Have I reason to fear you, Raf?' she countered, and saw a muscle at the edge of his jaw tighten infinitesimally before his expression was successfully masked.

'It depends on your connotation of the word,' he drawled with studied indolence.

The temptation to slap him was almost impossible to ignore, but she managed to school her features and present an unruffled expression. 'I fail to see why I should fall in with your plans.' In two years she'd spoken to him infrequently on the telephone, invariably about business matters, and the only personal touch had been expensive floral tributes, doubtless organised by his secretary, on her birthday and at Christmas.

'I'm sure your natural curiosity will overcome any reservations you might have.'

Oh, he was as infuriatingly *impossible* as ever! Chelsea decided, hating his level of assurance and the unswerving belief that she would accept. 'I already have a luncheon appointment,' she declared, determined to be assertive, and caught the gleam of amusement apparent as he met her defiant stare.

'Cancel it,' Raf insisted. 'Have your secretary book a table for two at midday. Somewhere close.'

'No.' She met his gaze fearlessly, and saw his eyes narrow in musing speculation

'Don't be so contentious, he chided quietly. 'It doesn't suit you.'

She felt like hitting him, and barely resisted the temptation as she raked his strong, masculine features, noting that the grooves that slashed his cheeks seemed deeper, the tiny lines fanning from his eyes more clearly defined. There were a few grey strands among the dark hair at his temples, adding a distinguished air that was oddly at variance with the harsh planes created by his well-defined bone structure. Physically, there appeared to be little change to his taut, steel-muscled body.

What had she expected? Chelsea pondered wryly. Evidence that Raf had discontinued a fitness programme which kept him at a physical and mental peak necessary to maintain his high-profile life-style? A silent laugh bubbled up inside her throat. The man was too formidably indomitable to allow anything to detract from his pursuit of power.

'Finished?'

The dry sound of his voice brought twin flags of colour to her cheeks, and she became trapped beneath his mocking appraisal.

How long had she been staring at him? No more than a few seconds, surely? 'Yes.' Incredible that she could sound so calm.

'Midday, Chelsea,' Raf reminded her with lazy tolerance. Then, turning, he walked a few paces, pulled open the door and stood aside for her to precede him from the room.

She made her exit with outward confidence, head held high, wearing a seemingly relaxed expression which totally belied her inner fragility. As she passed within touching distance she caught the faint muskiness of his cologne, and hated the way it teased her senses.

Then she was in the corridor, and seconds later she reached the sanctuary of her office, immeasurably relieved to be able to close herself temporarily away from super-sensitised eyes and ears within the Houghton-Hamilton organisation. Without doubt the whispers concerning Raf Hamilton's unannounced arrival would circulate and gather rapid, and probably erroneous, momentum. A weary grimace tugged the corner of Chelsea's attractively shaped mouth. It irked unbearably that her only defence was to display unruffled composure. Anything else would merely prove she was still susceptible to her husband's magnetic appeal.

Chelsea crossed to the plate-glass window to stand gazing sightlessly out over the harbour. Unconsciously she hugged her arms together, mindless of the rigid protectiveness of her stance.

Unbidden, the memories came flooding back, taunting, provocative, and unquestionably painful.

Years spent in exclusive boarding-schools had ensured that she had received the best education money could buy and, capped by a final year in Switzerland being fashionably 'finished', she returned home to complete a course in business management and to become her widowed father's social hostess, unwittingly pre-empting the steadily increasing succession of women in Sam Houghton's life. That some of her father's feminine partners were half his age and obviously enamoured of his wealth wasn't something she found easy to condone, but Sam enjoyed the superficial adoration and the pleasure he derived from their companionship. He was not sufficiently foolish, he assured her, to put a ring on any one of their fingers, and witnessing their ploys to become the second Mrs Houghton provided him with a wicked source of amusement.

A rapidly lengthening queue of hopeful young men began beating a path to *her* door, far more concerned with the Houghton millions than with *Chelsea* Houghton. Men whose earnest attention bore no significance in her life. Until the appearance of Raf Hamilton.

A slight tremor shook Chelsea's slim frame, and the curved tips of her fingernails dug mercilessly into the soft flesh of her arms, yet she felt no pain. She had been a pawn, she reflected bitterly, unable to forget or forgive the element of collusion between two skilled manipulators intent on forging a business empire, for there was no doubt in her mind that Raf's presence in her life had been as deliberately engineered as the delicate negotiations that merged Houghton with Hamilton.

With conscious reluctance Chelsea allowed her thoughts to wander back more than three years to the occasion of one of her father's glittering dinner parties held in the splendid dining-room of his gracious home. There were the usual twelve guests, a number deemed by Sam to be intimate enough to be interesting. She had no difficulty recalling the evening, or remembering precisely who was there, what she wore, the carefully selected menu. It was as if it were indelibly imprinted in her brain . . .

'Darling, come and be introduced to an associate of mine,' Sam told her the instant she emerged into the lounge, en route from the kitchen where she'd helped Hannah check the *hors d'oeuvre*. A minor domestic crisis had arisen early that afternoon when the girl Hannah usually employed to help out had telephoned to say she was confined to bed with a virulent virus.

'Raf Hamilton. My daughter, Chelsea.'

Chelsea sought a polite smile as she glanced towards the man her father introduced, and found herself held captive by a pair of riveting grey eyes.

Her own eyes widened fractionally, then assumed their customary warmth as she inclined her head in acknowledgement. 'Mr Hamilton.'

A smile tugged the egdes of his sensuously moulded mouth. 'Please, call me Raf.'

'Which is an abbreviation for . . .?' As an attempt at lightness, it merely deepened his smile and added a musing gleam to the depths of his eyes.

'Rafael.'

'Hmm.' Chelsea tilted her head slightly and regarded him with studied complacency. 'It suits you.'

There was an aura of power apparent in his projected image, as well as an indefinable quality that set him apart from any man she'd ever met before.

'I'm pleased you approve.' His voice was a deep, American-accent drawl, and succeeded in sending shivers down the length of her spine.

Somehow Sam had managed to fade away, and Chelsea glimpsed his profile from the periphery of her vision, noting absently that his latest conquest, Samantha, was attached to his side with the avidness of a clinging vine.

'One assumes your visit to Australia is not merely pleasure-orientated,' Chelsea remarked by way of polite conversation, and received a mocking averment.

'Your father is keen to do business with me.'

It made her look at him with renewed interest. As a shrewd corporate dealer, Sam had few equals among his associates. Yet Raf Hamilton was assuredly one, she perceived instinctively. Success emanated from his immaculately suited frame. If a battle of wills had to be fought, this man would undoubtedly emerge the winner.

For a brief few seconds she upbraided her own keen sense of insight, dismissing it as fanciful, and chose to resort to a singularly sweet smile. 'Dare I foresee a war of the Titans?'

His teeth gleamed as he broke into quiet laughter. 'I must ask Sam to seat you opposite me at dinner.'

'Good heavens, I feel distinctly honoured!' Her green eyes were totally lacking in guile, filled instead with answering amusement, and deep inside she was aware of a strange sense of excitement; a surge of blood coursing through her veins that made her feel almost light-headed.

Dinner was an anticlimax; successful, as were all

Sam's dinner parties, combining excellent cuisine and wine with stimulating social chatter. Chelsea excelled in her position as hostess, the epitome of natural charm and innate good manners.

'Such a pleasant child,' one guest murmured to Sam in a gesture of condescension at the close of the evening, and Chelsea barely managed to conceal a momentary flash of irritation.

It had never bothered her what Sam's guests thought, but tonight she didn't want to be considered anything remotely related to *child*, and *pleasant* seemed uninteresting and downright staid.

Unbidden, her gaze wandered to encounter a pair of amused grey eyes, and her pupils dilated at the faint mockery apparent in them. It seemed impossible to imagine that Raf Hamilton had successfully read her thoughts; totally embarrassing if he detected that *he* was the reason she wanted to appear a sophisticated woman of the world, attuned to the needs of man.

Not just *any* man, she thought hours later as she lay sleepless in bed, unsure whether she had been wise to accept his theatre invitation for the following evening.

Chelsea was ready when he arrived, dressed in a Bruce Oldfield designer original in pale aquamarine silk that clung lovingly to every curve, over which she'd added a matching beaded evening jacket. The colour complemented the texture of her honey-gold skin and highlighted her ash-blonde hair. Her make-up was minimal, with emphasis on her eyes, a skilful touch of blusher and careful application of lipstick. Perfume dabbed generously to every pulsebeat exuded the subtle tones of Chanel, elusive and tantalising in a teasing waft of exclusiveness.

She moved forward as Raf entered the lounge, greeting him with genuine warmth intermingled with a sense of hidden trepidation. He looked dangerous, the type of man the mother of any sensible girl would advise her daughter to stay away from—except she didn't have a mother to ask, and besides, there was a sense of the forbidden about him that was as potent as a powerful magnet.

'Hmm,' Raf drawled musingly as his eyes slowly encompassed her slim form. 'You look beautifully cool. Almost fragile.'

'Appearances can be deceptive,' Chelsea returned with the utmost solemnity. 'I'm really very durable.'

'I'm relieved to hear it.' A slight teasing smile twisted the edges of his mouth. 'Shall we leave?'

A sleek white limousine stood parked beneath the ornate portico with a uniformed chauffeur hovering solicitously beside an open rear door.

'We could have used my car,' Chelsea murmured as the vechicle slid out into the flow of traffic and cruised towards the city.

'I prefer to employ the hotel's limousine service whenever I'm away from the States,' Raf explained, and she turned towards him slowly, experiencing a strange tripping sensation in the accelerating beat of her heart.

'In that case, I shall simply sit back and relax,' she responded lightly, and glimpsed his faint smile.

The restaurant was one she'd frequented before, an élite establishment specialising in mouthwatering French cuisine, imported wines and impeccable service.

Throughout the meal Chelsea was supremely conscious of Raf's every glance, the warm, almost intimate smile he gave her whenever their eyes seemed to meet—which was often. Some form of elusive magic appeared to be pulling them together, and she felt immeasurably afraid. Raf Hamilton was a breed apart from the type of man she usually dated, and instinct warned that to become involved with him in any way would only be asking for heartache.

Afterwards she could not have recounted what topic of conversation they chose to discuss, nor could she clearly remember what she ate. And in the limousine, during what seemed to be an impossibly long drive home, she felt as nervous as a kitten, acutely attuned to his every move.

Had she been too gauche for him to want to ask her out again? Would he kiss her goodnight? A sudden shiver feathered the length of her spine at the thought of how his sensuously moulded lips might feel on her own.

When the limousine drew to a halt outside the main entrance of Sam's elegant mansion, Raf caught hold of her hand and lifted it to his lips in a strangely gentle gesture.

'Goodnight, Chelsea.' His voice was a soft, seductive drawl, and she melted into a thousand pieces, unsure what she uttered in response, if indeed she said anything at all as she stepped out from the large vehicle.

The telephone rang at eight the next morning as she was having breakfast on the terrace, and she *knew* who the caller was even before Hannah brought out the portable extension.

'If I can tie up this morning's business meeting by midday, will you join me for lunch? I thought we could spend the afternoon sightseeing.' Raf's voice lightened with amusement. 'A week in Sydney, and all I've seen of the city is the inside of numerous boardrooms during the day, and the interior of a variety of homes by night.'

Suddenly the day seemed brighter, the summer warmth an evocative caress on her sun-kissed skin, and she had to physically repress the light bubble of laughter that rose in her throat at the thought of spending several more hours in Raf Hamilton's company.

'On one condition,' Chelsea responded solemnly. 'No chauffeured limousine. We'll take my car. Unless,' she added impishly, 'your male ego will be irreparably shattered if I relegate you to the passenger seat.'

A dry chuckle reached down the line of her ears. 'I think it will survive.'

'We could take a picnic hamper to the beach,' she offered, then fell silent as she wondered if relaxing in the sun on the sandy foreshore was his idea of leisurely enjoyment.

'That sounds fine,' Raf said quietly. 'I'll call you when the meeting has finished.'

Chelsea collected him at his hotel shortly after midday and drove north to the Barranjoey Peninsula, selecting one of the picturesque coves that was more secluded than most for their picnic lunch.

Raf had chosen to wear casual shorts, a short-sleeved navy blue shirt, and she felt faintly bemused at the radical transformation from the impeccably suited businessman of the previous evening.

She had packed towels and a swimsuit, as well as a beach umbrella, and Hannah had provided them with a veritable feast, which, washed down with a glass of chilled white wine, became an epicurean delight.

Afterwards they packed everything back into the car, then strolled barefoot along the beach. A breeze had sprung up, its vicarious currents teasing the length of her hair and whipping the edges of her cotton skirt against her legs.

A gull soared overhead, its keen cry a solitary, sad sound in the silence that surrounded them. Chelsea watched its flight for long, enervating seconds as it glided effortlessly down to the sea.

'Perhaps we should turn back,' she suggested lightly, unwilling to commit herself. 'You requested a sightseeing tour, and there's a lot more to Sydney than an isolated northern cove.'

The remainder of the day held a magical quality as she drove through French's Forest before heading south-west and swinging east through the city itself towards Centennial Park. From there she took Raf on a scenic tour through Woollahra to Watson's Bay, then chose the New South Head Road to the Royal Botanic Gardens and the Opera House.

It was almost six o'clock when she deposited him outside the entrance to his hotel, and the warmth of his smile made the blood sing in her veins all the way home, where, after a shower and change of clothes, she joined Sam for dinner, then watched television before opting for an early night.

She woke to the swishing sound of curtains being opened, and the delicious aroma of freshly made coffee.

'What time is it?' She slid out of bed and viewed Hannah with wry resignation on being informed it was after ten. 'That late?' She reached for her robe and slipped it on. 'You should have woken me.'

'You're on vacation,' Hannah demurred as she moved towards the door. 'After studying hard all year and passing every exam with honours, you deserve some relaxation.'

Perhaps there was some logic in Hannah's observation, Chelsea reflected as she sipped her coffee minutes later, deciding a day spent in solitude sunbathing on the beach with a book would provide all the relaxation she required.

An hour later she lay supine beneath a beach umbrella, a weighty paperback in hand and with soothing music emerging from a portable transistor.

When she returned home there was a message from Sam requesting that she meet him at five at Lloyd and Patti Lumsden's Seaforth residence. A cocktail party, Hannah elaborated.

Quite why her father wanted her to go was a mystery, Chelsea thought wryly as she sipped her second glass of mineral water and attempted to appear totally absorbed in Lloyd junior's self-lauding appraisal of his escalating climb within his father's industrial empire. Especially when Sam had one of his latest conquests very clearly in tow. Then she caught sight of a familiar dark head on the far side of the room, and her heart quickened its beat.

Raf Hamilton, in conversation with not one but

two beautiful women. Almost as if he sensed her gaze, his eyes swept to encompass hers, and she glimpsed the slightly quizzical lift of one eyebrow, saw his smile, which she acknowledged before returning her attention to the unctuous Lloyd junior who hadn't even noticed the digression of her attention.

She wanted to slip away, but where?

'You will come, won't you?'

Chelsea registered the words and cast the junior Lloyd a suitably regretful glance. 'No, I'm afraid not.'

'Good evening,' a deep voice drawled from close behind, and she turned to see Raf Hamilton standing within touching distance, his features assembled into a polite mask.

The younger man fairly bristled with indignation, and could be seen to visibly size his opponent and ignore every warning sign not to proceed. 'Chelsea, do you know this man?'

Chelsea politely effected an introduction, then watched in idle fascination as Raf made no attempt to engage the younger man in conversation and, seconds later Lloyd strode off in an angry huff.

'Another drink?' Raf calmly took her empty glass and beckoned a hovering waiter.

'I don't want any more.'

'Nor do I,' Raf drawled. 'Let's get out of here.'

'We can't leave!' She felt vaguely scandalised, and watched as he placed their glasses on the waiter's tray.

His eyes held hers. 'In another hour everyone will be gone.'

'Sam——'

'Knows you're with me.'

'I'm not *with* you,' she began, only to come to a halt as he pressed a gentle forefinger over her lips.

'*Yes.*'

Chelsea closed her eyes, then opened them again. 'Why?' Her gaze was remarkably clear, steady, when inside every nerve-end seemed to stretch to its farthest limitation.

'We both need to eat.' His smile was lazy and extended to the depth of his eyes. 'Why not together?'

A refusal would sound churlish, and besides, she was hungry. 'In that case, thank you.'

Raf directed the limousine to a charming restaurant in Double Bay where they dined in splendour on succulent seafood and drank fine wine, then they danced very close to soft, dreamy music.

It felt so *right*, she didn't pull away when he enfolded her completely into his arms and rested his cheek down against her own.

'It must be late,' she murmured uneasily almost an hour later as he paid the bill and escorted her out to the waiting limousine.

The look he thrust her was swift and analytical, and the butterflies in Chelsea's stomach set up a frightening beat as she slipped into the rear seat, aware that Raf followed close behind. After giving the driver her address, he reached for her hand and held it loosely within his own.

Chelsea thought of a dozen things to say, and discarded each as sounding completely inane. Instead she gazed sightlessly ahead, barely registering the bright city neon lights or the passing traffic.

It was difficult to remain calm with his thumb caressing the delicate veins at her wrist. In the semi-darkness of the limousine she was incredibly aware of him, her senses heightened to such a degree that she had to make a conscious effort to breathe evenly, and she felt a surge of relief when the vehicle slid to a halt beneath the brightly lit portico.

A few polite words framed her lips as she turned towards Raf, but they never found voice. His mouth was close, so close that she was momentarily locked into immobility.

Quite what she had expected, she wasn't sure. Certainly not the open-mouthed gentleness with which he captured her lips, nor the provocative, teasing caress of his kiss. A shaft of exquisite longing unfurled deep within until her body became alive, aching for his touch. She began to tremble and felt her defences crumble into an ignominious heap. It would be so easy to wind her arms round his neck and kiss him back, yet she sat still, deliberately passive, and felt strangely bereft as he lifted his head and reached for the clasp to unlatch her door.

'Goodnight, Chelsea.' His voice bore a trace of mockery, and she slid out from the car and let herself into the house without so much as a backward glance.

For some unknown reason she wanted to cry. He hadn't said he'd ring, nor had he arranged to see her again. As she undressed ready for bed, she told herself she didn't care, but the telltale ache in the region of her heart proved a betrayal.

With the dawn came reason and a determination

to put the compelling Raf Hamilton completely out of her mind. Chelsea rose early and stroked numerous vigorous lengths of the pool before showering and changing for breakfast, then she telephoned a few friends and arranged to meet them for lunch. The decision to embark on a shopping expedition would fill in the empty hours, and she drove into the city intent on adding to her extensive wardrobe, returning at six o'clock considerably cheered by the purchase of three new outfits, a stimulating luncheon, and the indulgence of a body massage and facial at her favourite beauty salon.

'Darling, you look gorgeous,' Sam greeted her as she entered the lounge half an hour later. 'Your usual Perrier? Or will you be reckless and join me in a glass of champagne?'

'Hmm.' She pretended to give the choice serious thought. 'Champagne, if we're meant to be celebrating something.' Her nose wrinkled with impish humour. 'Am I to be informed of the occasion, or is it a deep, intimate secret?'

Her father's laughter sounded low and husky and full of genuine amusement. 'Just a business deal that I have every confidence will be successful.'

She raised an inquisitive eyebrow as she accepted the slim crystal flute from his hand. 'In that case, isn't this a bit premature?'

'Not at all, darling,' Sam assured her with droll cynicism. 'Negotiations have been completed and I have a signed option.'

Chelsea lifted her glass in a silent toast, then sipped the excellent Bollinger. 'Congratulations.'

Her father inclined his head, then met her sparkling

glance. 'Shall we take *Mystique* out and cruise the Hawkesbury for the weekend?'

'Just the two of us?' It was almost too much to ask, for Sam's twenty-metre cruiser was luxuriously fitted, slept eight as well as two crew, and was often host to numerous business and pleasure functions.

Sam shrugged, then shot her a warm smile. 'Anyone in particular you'd like to ask?'

'Aside from you? No.'

'Ah, now that's what I call familial devotion!' He leant forward and bestowed a kiss to her temple. 'I love you too, darling. More champagne?'

Why not? What was more, Chelsea sipped a third glass with dinner, and slept like a baby to wake refreshed and eager for the weekend ahead.

Mystique lay moored to the jetty at the bottom of their garden, and Chelsea boarded early, helping Hannah store supplies while Will ran a last-minute mechanical check prior to departure.

The powerful throb of engines heralded Sam's arrival, and Chelsea moved quickly into her cabin and unpacked—a simple task, as she had only brought a change of shorts and a top, a bikini, a dress for dinner, and the usual lingerie and toiletries.

She could hear voices as she emerged and made her way back up on the deck, and there was the sound of her father's laughter mingling with a slightly deeper male drawl that needed no verification to identify its owner. Raf Hamilton, looking incredibly fit and tanned in casual white shorts and a sleeveless top, and whose smile on greeting her was slow and warm and infinitely lazy.

Why did she suddenly feel as if a minor hurricane

had swept through her emotions and whipped them into a state of turmoil?

It took considerable effort to present a relaxed façade as she turned to welcome Gabrielle and Henri Bisset on board. Friends of long standing, the charming French couple were convivial company, and Chelsea viewed their inclusion with a degree of relief.

Within minutes *Mystique* eased away from the jetty, gradually picking up speed as Will guided her expertly towards the Spit.

There were a number of motorised craft cruising the inner harbour, for the weather was glorious, warm sunshine tempered by a slight sea breeze, and Chelsea followed Gabrielle's example in applying sunblock to every visible area of exposed skin.

'Allow me,' a deep voice drawled from behind as she attempted to smooth lotion on her back, and there was little she could do by way of protest when the plastic bottle was taken from her nerveless fingers. His touch was gentle yet firm, and sent shivers scudding in countless different directions as he completed the task.

Wayward thoughts entered her brain, causing havoc with her nervous system as she contemplated what it would be like if she was completely alone with him.

A stupid crush, that's all it is, Chelsea dismissed minutes later as she thanked him politely and moved to join Gabrielle at the railing. He's merely a very physically presentable man with more than his fair share of dynamic masculinity, she assured herself, adding with inherent honesty that there was nothing blatant or overt in his manner; just a wary, cynical acceptance, perhaps, of his effect on the opposite sex.

Damn! What had begun as a carefree weekend looked like being fraught with numerous tensions —even if they were entirely of her own making—and she cursed Sam afresh for putting her in such an untenable position. For the next thirty hours she would be thrown into inescapable contact with the disturbing Raf Hamilton; a prospect she viewed with considerable apprehension, for she doubted her ability to emerge unscathed.

Unless Sam diverted from his usual course, they would anchor for the night near Gosford and dine at the Yacht Club, cruise the Hawkesbury River the following morning after a leisurely breakfast on board, weigh anchor for a few hours in order to cast out fishing-lines, then slowly make their way back home before nightfall.

Which was precisely what eventuated, and afterwards Chelsea wondered if she'd dreamed the veiled warmth in the depths of Raf's eyes, the slight lingering touch of his hand at her elbow when he helped her disembark at Gosford. Perhaps her fevered imaginatin was to blame for likening him to a stalking tiger sure of its prey, content to stay at a distance, yet close enough to make his presence known.

If that was his strategy, it succeeded, for her awareness of him became heightened to such a degree that she was conscious of his every move, and she found herself examining everything he said for any hidden nuance that might provide the key to his intentions.

Intentions! She had to be mad. What would

someone like Raf Hamilton want with her?

Yet he accepted Sam's invitation to dine on their return to Castlecrag, while Gabrielle and Henri elected to decline, and Chelsea was even more confused at the end of the evening when her father brushed aside Raf's request to call a taxi.

'Nonsense! Chelsea will drive you into the city, won't you, darling?'

Being the focus of two pairs of male eyes, one convinced of her acquiescence, the other merely faintly amused, strengthened her resolve to agree—if only to prove that it was simply an act of good manners.

Her gaze was quite steady as she glanced towards Raf. 'Of course.' She even managed a polite smile. 'If you'll excuse me, I'll just collect my keys.'

In the car she drove with admirable competence, considering the state of her nerves, and she refrained from conversing for the sake of it, preferring instead to concentrate on the evening traffic as they neared the city.

'Will you share a coffee with me?'

The question took her unawares, and she was momentarily lost for an answer. 'Where?'

'My hotel.'

Oh, heavens! Her breath seemed to lock inside her throat, and it was to her credit that she didn't grate the gears as she shifted into first and cleared the intersection.

'I had one of the downstairs lounges in mind,' Raf drawled. 'Not my suite.'

Only an attempt at facetious humour would save her from complete disaster. 'Good heavens, what a delightful change from——' she paused fractionally to mimic'—''come up and see my etchings''!' Now she could afford to be merciless. 'Or is it ''financial portfolio'' these days?'

His response was an echo of silent laughter, bringing an answering smile to her lips.

'Coffee, Chelsea. For now.'

Why did she feel postively *threatened* by those last two words? 'Thanks—but no, thanks,' she responded quietly as she slid the car into the entrance bay immediately adjacent to his hotel and brought it to a halt.

'Next time,' Raf mused, taking in her clear-eyed resolve with a narrowed, slightly speculative gaze. With calm deliberation he leaned forward and bestowed a brief, hard kiss on her unsuspecting lips, then he opened the passenger door and slid out before she could regain her breath.

The following afternoon brought the delivery of a magnificent sheaf of red roses, no message, just a slashing signature on the accompanying card, and what was supposed to be a quiet dinner at home on her own became dinner *à deux* with Raf's stated invited arrival mere minutes before Hannah was due to serve her meal. At a dining-table set for two, Chelsea observed as she took her seat.

It was true Sam had telephoned late that afternoon to say he would be unavoidably delayed and not to wait dinner, but he'd made no mention of having invited Raf as a guest. A genuine slip, or deliberate subterfuge?

'Thank you for the roses,' Chelsea said politely as she toyed with the appetising avocado vinaigrette, and glimpsed his slow smile.

The main course was a delicious *filet mignon* with

fresh-cooked vegetables, but she forked only a few mouthfuls before pushing the plate to one side.

'Coffee?' Was it obvious she was so nervous in his presence?

His gaze beneath dark-fringed lashes was curiously intent and watchful, and she looked at him carefully.

'I fail to understand why you constantly seek my company.'

'You're a beautiful young woman,' Raf declared quietly. 'With intelligence and integrity. Why shouldn't I want to spend time with you?'

'Because I'm not in your league,' she said simply, and his low smile was warm and infinitely lazy as he reached out and caught hold of her hand.

'Come and show me the view of the harbour,' he ordered. 'I caught a glimpse of it the last time I was here.'

Without a word she allowed him to lead her out on to the patio, coming to a halt as they reached the balustraded edge of the swimming pool.

Pinpricks of far-distant stars appeared as a minuscule reflection of the neon city lights, with brilliant flashing signs in a variety of colours vying for supremacy against a backdrop of fully lit office blocks as teams of cleaners worked into the night.

'Breathtaking!'

Chelsea glanced towards him and saw that his attention was centred on her, not the panoramic vista in the distance.

She stookd completely still as his hand captured her chin, taking it between thumb and forefinger and lifting it so she had little choice but to look at him.

Her lashes lowered in self-defence, but there was nothing she could do about the faint trembling of her mouth.

'For goodness' sake, please don't look like that,' Raf directed softly, then his head lowered and his mouth settled on hers with gentle possession.

Chelsea felt her body shiver with reaction as a slow heat coursed through her veins, bringing alive a multitude of sensations she was loath to define. All that mattered was *now*, and the singing, pulsing awareness that made her totally malleable in his arms.

Without warning, the gentleness underwent a subtle change as he moulded her close, and she felt as if she was transported body and soul on to an illusory sensory plateau from which she never wanted to descend.

Then she was free, and she could only look at him wordlessly, unable to conjure a single rational thought.

His eyes were dark with a deep, slumbrous warmth, and his mouth curved into a slight smile as he lifted a hand to tuck a wayward tendril of hair back behind her ear. 'You offer a man a touch of paradise, do you know that?'

Was it so wrong to want a total satiation of the senses, the flesh? To deny every moral conviction she had ever possessed?

'I think you'd better leave.' Her voice sounded shaky, even to her own ears, and oddly forlorn.

'Is it me you're afraid of, or what I represent?' *Both*, she longed to cry. But worst of all, I'm afraid of myself.

'I'm due in Los Angeles at the end of next week.'

So soon? Her heart felt as if it had taken a sudden massive blow. Somehow it seemed incredibly important to present a light-hearted appearance. 'I hope you've enjoyed your stay,' she offered, aware that inside she was breaking into a thousand pieces.

'I'd like you to come back with me.'

Her expressive features registered an entire gamut of emotions as she struggled to contain them. 'You can't be serious?' she uttered faintly, unable to glance away from him if her life depended on it.

'Perfectly serious,' Raf assured her, adding softly, 'As my wife.'

Shocked surprise momentarily robbed her of speech. 'I've only known you a short time,' she breathed shakily, her eyes wide pools of incredulity. 'How can I?' Even as she uttered the words, others more important vied for supremacy. 'What will Sam think?'

'Your father has already given his blessing,' Raf told her gently, drawing her close within the circle of his arms.

She felt as if she'd been tossed high into the air, and unsure if she could land on her feet.

'Are you going to refuse me?'

'No,' Chelsea declared unsteadily, lifting her eyes to meet his. 'Won't you give me more time to get used to the idea? A week isn't long enough to arrange a wedding, or——'

'Believe me, everything will be exactly as it should be.'

And it was. From her wedding dress to the three-tiered cake, and the guests, but most reassuring of all was Sam's obvious delight in the entire event.

Even the thought of living on the other side of the world didn't worry her, and after a honeymoon in France she had attempted to settle into married life with a husband who jetted from one State to another with such frequency, he maintained apartments in three key cities as well as a palatial hillside residence overlooking Los Angeles.

As a lover, Raf surpassed every romantic fantasy she'd ever indulged, but it wasn't long before she became riddled with doubt regarding his feelings for her. Feminine socialites, young and not so young, openly coveted the man at her side, often with such a blatant disregard for her presence that Chelsea found it difficult to disguise her embarrassment, not to mention containing her anger. He exuded a dramatic mesh of male sexuality and power, making it all too easy to cast him in the same wheeling-dealing-executive mould as her father. She began to feel afraid she would end up as her mother had—a decorative piece of Dresden china brought out on show for each social function, then neglected until the next occasion her services were required as her husband's hostess.

With the doubts came the arguments. Heated discussions on Chelsea's part, cool rationale from Raf. She began to refuse to accompany him on business trips, contrarily welcoming yet hating his absence. There were also a few vicious rumours circulating among the social set, the most distressing of all relating to the real reason Raf had married her—namely the business merger of Houghton and Hamilton being sealed privately with a marriage of convenience.

On the eve of their first wedding anniversary she received news that Sam had been hospitalised pending extensive surgery from which he never recovered.

Her father's death had resulted in a terrible sense of loss, and consumed with grief she had insisted on remaining in Sydney when Raf flew back to America a week after the funeral.

The gossip columinsts had a field day, speculating about their separation, and a month later Raf had issued an ultimatum to the effect that unless she rejoined him in the States the next move must be *hers*.

Weeks became months as she began taking an interest in Houghton-Hamilton, excelling in the challenge of assuming an inherited directorship, and, the longer the parting from Raf, the more difficult it became to attempt to bridge the gap.

The thought of an inevitable confrontation was something she had pushed to the back of her mind. Until now.

CHAPTER THREE

A MUTED beep from the intercom on Chelsea's desk interrupted her reflection, and she shivered with involuntary reaction as she crossed to answer its summons.

'Yes, Susan. What is it?'

'I require confirmation of a two-thirty appointment with Rosemount. I have him on hold on the other line. Will you be back from lunch in time?'

A quick glance at her watch revealed that it was almost midday. 'Yes, of course.' Whatever was Susan thinking of? She'd never taken a two-and-a-half-hour lunch break that was unrelated to business. Then she remebered. Raf.

Dammit! Now she'd *have* to go out to lunch. But not to a restaurant; she'd pick up some sandwiches and a drink and take them to a nearby park. A picnic snack eaten al fresco would be something of a novelty. And, if she was quick enough, she'd be out of the building before Raf became aware of her absence.

Chelsea entered the elevator and reached the downstairs foyer without incident, where she collected a magazine and something to eat from a nearby lunch bar prior to crossing the park.

It was hot outside, the reflected heat from the pavement merely accentuating the high midsummer temperature, and it was a relief to find seating space beneath one of several shady trees dotting the picturesque reserve.

There was a number of people idling away their lunch hour, some in groups, couples, a few on their own engrossed in a book or listening to music through a transistorised headset as they ate a packed lunch, Chelsea observed before she shifted her attention to her magazine and began leafing idly through its pages.

Her appetite seemed to have disappeared, and after a few perfunctory bites she discarded the sandwich in favour of the bottle of fruit juice, which was fresh and icy and exactly what she needed to quench her thirst.

Attired in a designer original dress, imported Italian shoes, impeccable make-up, an equally impeccable hairstyle and wearing expensive jewellery, she looked and felt incredibly out of place.

'Mind if I join you?'

Chelsea slowly raised her head to meet a pair of dark eyes regarding her with something akin to cynical amusement. She hadn't heard his footfall, nor sensed his impending presence. Perhaps her sensory antennae had gone into a state of shock upon his initial arrival and needed a recovery period, she decided wryly.

'Do I have a choice?'

'Not really,' Raf returned smoothly as he lowered his lengthy frame down on to the seat beside her.

'Are you monitoring my movements?' Her gaze was remarkably direct, almost accusatory. 'I refuse to believe your appearance here is merely conincidental.'

His eyes locked with hers, their expression unfathomable, and she suppressed a faint, shivery sensation, aware of his sheer masculinity and the threat he posed to her equilibrium.

'I was standing at the window in Jonathan's office when I saw you cross the street.'

'Therefore deducing that I wouldn't be meeting you for lunch,' Chelsea remarked coolly, fixing her attention on a distant pedestrian in a bid to remain calm.

Raf stretched an arm along the back of the seat, and she was supremely conscious of his hand within touching distance of her shoulder.

The edge of his mouth lifted in silent mockery. 'I regarded it in the nature of a request.'

'Which I chose to decline.' She felt defensive, almost like a recalcitrant child up against an authoritarian adult—an effect Raf was able to evoke without any effort at all, she decided ruefully.

'We could have shared a meal in air-conditioned comfort, rather than an impromptu picnic in the midday heat.'

She turned her head to look at him, refusing to admit that the flipping sensation in her stomach was due to anything other than indigestion. 'Why, Raf,' she began sweetly, 'is slumming it on a park bench beneath your dignity?'

For a moment his eyes gleamed with anger, and his voice when he spoke was dangerously soft. 'I'd advise putting a curb on your tongue, Chelsea. You're way out of your depth.'

With some difficulty she caught hold of her temper, choosing silence rather than voluble rage.

'Thank you.' There was faint mockery evident,

and her eyes flashed vividly in response, hating the musing cynicism, the degree of self-assurance that put him far ahead of any man she'd ever met.

'Perhaps you'd care to dispense with the veil of secrecy and tell me why you've decided to visit Sydney,' she invited in stilted tones.

'Presumably you won't choose to hazard a guess?'

'Why should I play a game in which you have all the answers?' she countered coolly. A prickle of apprehension tightened her skin as a number of differing conclusions raced through her brain. Aside from business, she could only think of one personal reason for Raf's presence and, although she'd given the possibility some thought on a number of occasions over the past two years, now suddenly it rose up in front of her like Nemesis.

He was silent for so long, she didn't have the courage to look at him, let alone attempt to bridge the ensuing silence.

Time hung like a suspended entity, and she became aware of every breath she took, deliberately regulating each separate one in an attempt to look unruffled. *Damn*! The silent curse died in her throat. Why should she be so affected by him, just when she'd begun to reconcile herself to enjoying the control she'd established over her life? Within the space of minutes of his reappearance—seconds, she amended grimly—he'd dispensed with every barrier she'd erected against him. It wasn't fair.

'As you are aware,' he went on smoothly, 'when Hamilton merged with Houghton, a thirty per cent stake in the company was made available to the public through a float on the stock market. The remaining seventy per cent was held equally between Sam and myself, with Sam's share inherited by you on his death.' He paused fractionally, and she sat still, unwilling to say as much as a word until he was through.

'Over the past month, a single buyer has been purchasing as many shares as possible, lifting the price way above par. If he were able to persuade you to part with a major parcel of your shares, it would give him a monopoly.'

'No one has approached me,' Chelsea revealed slowly.

'Not yet.'

'I wouldn't sell, anyway,' she assured him gravely, only too aware of the effort her father had put into founding the company and ensuring that it prospered.

'He could make an offer he considers you wouldn't refuse,' Raf said hardily. 'He might think that after a two-year separation, you might conceivably opt for divorce and therefore prefer to sever your ties with Houghton-Hamilton.'

If it was his intention to shock, he succeeded. Chelsea couldn't deny that she'd contemplated the possiblity of divorce, but always with Raf the instigator, never her.

'I see.'

'Do you, Chelsea?'

He sounded impossibly cynical, and it rankled unbearably. 'Oh, yes,' she said evenly. 'As it's one of your business ventures, the solidarity of Houghton-Hamilton must be protected at all costs.'

A tiny muscle clenched at the edge of his jaw, and

his eyelids lowered fractionally, successfully masking his expression. 'With that in mind, I take it I can count on your support?'

Why did she suddenly feel so—*intimidated*? Aware, instinctively, that she had managed to skate dangerously close to thin ice? Yet there was no basis for hesitancy. 'Of course.'

His lips twisted slightly, then parted to reveal strong white teeth. 'An unequivocable accedence, Chelsea?'

She found herself looking at him carefully, noting the powerful features, his direct, unwavering gaze. For a moment she was prey to a host of memories —how it felt to have that sensuously moulded mouth cover her own, the feel of his hand on her body, touching, caressing all the pleasure pulses . . . Pursuing such a train of thought was madness, and with considerable effort she centred her attention on the knot of his impeccable silk tie.

'Where the welfare of Houghton-Hamilton is at stake—yes.' Even to her own ears her voice sounded stiff and almost formal.

Something flickered in the depths of his eyes for an infinitesimal second before it was successfully hidden. 'Thank you.' Lifting a hand, he indicated the remains of her lunch. 'Do you intend finishing that?'

For a moment she looked startled, then she shook her head and handed him the partly eaten sandwich. 'It's chicken salad.'

His smile was slow and indolent. 'It will suffice for now.'

Chelsea watched in idle fascination as he took a generous bite, then his gaze trapped hers and she felt every single hair on her body prickle with inexplicable foreboding.

'If you'll excuse me?' she said as she rose gracefully to her feet. 'I have a lot of paperwork which needs my attention.'

'I'm sure it can wait.'

It could, but she doubted her ability to remain seated beside him for much longer without betraying how much his presence affected her. Even if she was able to present an outward air of calm, there was nothing she could do to disguise the rapidly beating pulse at the base of her throat.

'Yes.' Somehow she managed to hold his studied gaze. 'But with the onset of Christmas . . .' She allowed her voice to trail off as she gave a light shrug. 'Besides,' she added lightly, centring her attention on the empty lunch wrapping, 'you should get something substantial to eat. I rather doubt that half a sandwich has sated your appetite.'

A faint smile tugged the edges of his mouth, and the expression in his eyes was wholly cynical. 'Ah,' he murmured with deliberate mockery, 'how reassuring to discover you haven't forgotten my appetite!'

His implication was intentional, and Chelsea was powerless to prevent the telltale tide of pink that flooded her cheeks.

How could she forget? *Remembering* kept her awake at nights. Yet to acknowledge as much would be tantamount to an admission of sorts, and she refused to give him that satisfaction.

'I was referring to food,' she retorted, impossibly angry with herself for her careless choice of words.

'Of course,' he drawled.

Damn him! He had the ability to take anything she said and twist it any way he chose. Perhaps he'd missed his true vocation, she decided vengefully. As a barrister in a court of law, he'd be diabolical.

Without a further word she tucked her handbag beneath her arm, then she turned and walked away from him, uncaring whether he followed or not.

She hadn't covered more than a few metres before he fell into step beside her, and she determinedly remained aloof—not that it mattered at all, for he didn't utter so much as a word until they had left the tree-studded park and crossed to the opposite side of the road.

'Chelsea.'

She paused and looked at him carefully, barely registering the faint teasing gleam in the depths of his dark eyes as he leant forward and gently brushed his lips against her slightly parted, unsuspecting mouth.

'*Au revoir*.'

At least ten words in condemnation rose and died in her throat before she eventually uttered *one*, and by then it was too late, for Raf's retreating figure had moved out of earshot.

It didn't prevent the silent censure she heaped on his head as she stepped through the wide glass doors of the downstairs entrance foyer, and throughout the remainder of the afternoon it became impossible to dispel an intuitive feeling that he was intent on playing some kind of manipulative game.

It was after five when she put down her pen, closed the folder and slid it into the master file ready for Susan to return the following day. Her head ached, a dull, intensive heaviness that was broken every now and again by a team of minature tormentors armed with tiny sledgehammers who beat a painful symphony in the vicinity of her right temple. Even her neck and shoulders drooped with weariness, and she felt infinitely fragile in body and spirit.

The thought of facing the hustle of traffic-choked intersections during the drive home was sufficient to bring forth a faint groan, and for a few brief seconds she contemplated leaving her car overnight while she took a taxi to Castlecrag. Except that the possibility of securing one in under thirty minutes at this time of evening would be miraculous. She could, of course, ring Hannah and have Will drive in and collect her. The latter would provide no problem at all, yet she hesitated, all too aware that if she opted for Will's services it would be at least an hour before she reached home.

With a sigh of resignation she stretched her arms above her head and flexed her shoulders, then she rose to her feet, collected her briefcase and handbag, and vacated her office for the elevator and ultimately the underground car park.

The traffic was as bad, if not worse, than she'd anticipated, and twice the sleek lines of her Porshe came within a hair's breadth of an aggressively driven vehicle whose driver was totally oblivious to due care or consideration. It merely added to her level of tension, and by the time she eventually swung into her driveway all she could think of was the need for a long, cool glass of fresh fruit juice, a leisurely soak in scented bathwater, followed by a light snack, then bed.

Chelsea felt a surge of relief as she eased the car to-

wards the crest of the circular driveway, only to utter
a silent curse at the sight of an unfamiliar Jaguar
parked adjacent to the wide portico. A rental car, she
perceived as she waked past. Visitors, singular or
plural, were the last thing she needed at what she
had hoped was the end of a particularly traumatic
day. Yet it *was* the festive season, and she couldn't
dismiss the possibility that one of her out-of-State
friends had called in briefly to deliver a gift—
something she herself must do without too much
delay, she concluded with a faint smile as she
brought the Porsche to a halt close to the entrance.

Sheikh, the Alsation, bounded to greet her the
instant she emerged from the car, and his welcome
was seconded with double fervour as she entered the
house, where two adorable long-haired bundles
raced each other across the marble-tilted foyer in an
effort to be first to launch themselves into her arms.

'Ming, Pasha—that's enough!' Chelsea protested
as she hugged their wriggling bodies and attempted
to quieten their exuberant affection before releasing
them down on to the floor where they sat panting,
faces expectantly raised in anticipation of her next
move. 'Off you go outside,' she bade gently,
knowing she could count on their obedience. 'I have
visitors.'

Tails wagging, they immediately turned and
padded towards an open door which led to the rear of
the house.

Chelsea straightened and smoothed a hand over
the skirt of her dress, debating whether or not she
had time to freshen her make-up and tug a brush
through her hair before going into the lounge, when

Hannah appeared in the foyer looking distinctly flustered.

'Chelsea, I've been trying to reach you at the office, then on the mobile car phone.'

'Good heavens, has a major disaster occurred?' Chelsea attempted to keep her voice light, but there was an underlying element of concern beneath her natural curiosity, a vague but worrying feeling of apprehension that had seemed part of her for most of the day. Ever since Raf had made his unannounced appearance, a wretched voice whispered inside her brain.

'No, no,' the housekeeper reassured her quickly. 'Nothing has happened. It's just——' She hesitated momentarily, then rushed on quickly, 'Mr Hamilton arrived a short while ago.'

Raf was *here*? But then, why shouldn't he be? Chelsea registered dully. Sam, in his infinite wisdom, had bequeathed his home to his daughter *and* son-in-law, and she had never thought to contest his decision.

'I thought you'd appreciate some advance warn— notice,' Hannah corrected hurriedly, her kindly features creased with concern, and Chelsea gathered her wits together.

'It's all right, Hannah. Raf called into the office this morning.' If Oscars were being handed out for acting ability, she surely deserved a nomination!

Never once had she discussed her marriage with anyone, and when questioned about their apparent separation over the past two years she'd merely smiled and adroitly steered the conversation in another direction. No matter what speculation abounded, their relationship presented itself as a puzzling enigma, inevitably fired with confusion by the floral tributes that arrived twice a year. And, as Susan and Hannah could testify, Chelsea took a number of infrequent transatlantic telephone calls. Only Chelsea knew they were merely duty calls and that her conversation with Raf were mainly related to business.

'I had Will take his luggage upstairs,' Hannah voiced a trifle awkwardly as she caught her hands together, and her eyes clouded with genuine concern. 'The suite adjoining yours.' Now she looked distinctly uncomfortable. 'I wasn't sure, I wanted to check with you first.'

Chelsea felt the colour drain from her face. *Luggage.* Raf actually intended staying here? It was bad enough that he was in Sydney, but to have him sleep under the same roof . . .

'What time would you like me to serve dinner?'

Chelsea heard Hannah's query, but it seeemed to take several seconds before the words registered. With a mental shake she gathered her composure and met her housekeeper's troubled gaze. 'I'm not very hungry,' she said quietly, and forced herself to ask, 'Where's Raf?'

'Upstairs, taking a shower.' Hannah reached out a hand, then let it fall helplessly down at her side. 'Are you all right? You look terribly pale.'

Oh, lord, she'd have to get a grip on herself. 'Just . . .' she paused, and summoned up a shaky smile. 'Very tired. It's been a trying day.'

Hannah looked on the point of saying something, but instead held her peace, and Chelsea felt infinitely relieved. The housekeeper and her husband had been in residence for as long as she could remember, and were regarded as valued friends. During the past two years they had become increasingly protective of her welfare and, while Sam had been a caring parent, Hannah and Will were the mainstay of her existence.

The house was a beautifully spacious home, graciously furnished with priceless antiques, elegant pieces of furniture set against rich cream papered walls, soft-piled eau-de-Nil carpet, and toning curtains. Expensive art graced the walls, and crystal chandeliers hung suspended from ornately plastered ceilings.

'I'll freshen up, and change for dinner,' Chelsea decided, then made her way towards the wide central staircase.

Resentment at Raf's highhandedness fuelled her anger, and on reaching the upper floor she was determined to initiate a confrontation and demand an explanation of his presence here—insist that he remove himself and his luggage to a hotel.

At the very least he could reveal precisely *why* he had chosen not to enlighten her during lunch of his intention to move in, she seethed as she reached the hallway.

Her bedroom was large and formed part of three adjoining suites situated at the rear of the house overlooking the pool and gardens with a splendid view of Sailor's Bay, the Spit—and the Pacific Ocean could be glimpsed in the distance beyond the Sound.

The suite held particular significance in that it had been used by her mother, who, possessing a frail state of health, had preferred not to share a room with Sam, and to accommodate her wishes he had carried out renovations to all three suites facing the eastern side of the house, turning the middle suite into a comfortable sitting-room. He had taken the adjoining suite as his own, with connecting doors installed. For the past two years Chelsea had used her mother's set of rooms, unwilling for some inexplicable reason to utilise the suite she'd occupied prior to her own marriage. Pleasantly uncluttered, this suite was none the less essentially feminine, with capacious wardrobe space and an adjoining en-suite bathroom which was a sybaritic joy.

It had never been necessary for any of the doors to carry a lock, and consequently there was nothing to bar her entry to the bedroom Raf was planning to use.

In fact, she was so deeply angry, she didn't even bother to knock. Not that it mattered in the slightest, she discovered, for Raf wasn't even in the bedroom, although his clothes were very much in evidence across the bed, others hanging in the wardrobe, and a half-unpacked suitcase rested on a nearby velvet-padded rosewood stool. The door leading into his en-suite was partly open, and she could hear the shower running.

Damn, now she would have to wait. But not here, a tiny voice taunted. Any minute that shower was going to stop, and she needed every advantage she could get to parry his highly skilled verbal warfare. Being confronted by a naked male body was hardly conducive to conducting the type of questioning she had in mind!

Turning swiftly, she crossed back to her own room and slipped off her shoes, then she extracted fresh underwear and moved into her own bathroom, where she turned on the taps of the spa-bath before removing her clothes.

It was heaven to step into the gently pulsing water, and sheer bliss to sink into its scented depths. Its relaxing effect was almost immediate as it eased tired, taut muscles and gradually lulled her into a state of inertia.

She lay there for as long as she dared, then emerged to towel herself dry before completing her toilette and slipping a silk robe over her underwear.

Make-up was deliberately understated, just the merest brush of blusher, a soft shade of eyeshadow, and a pale pink gloss over her lips.

Choosing what to wear took a little more time, for she wanted something that wasn't too dressy, not too casual, in no way resembling anything like the tailored designer clothes she wore to the office. A waspish imp taunted that she should wear shorts and a T-shirt, and be damned! She was tempted to do just that, except that Raf would immediately judge such apparel at the dinner-table as an act of defiance and be amused. No—smart-casual was the look she coveted, and after much deliberation she selected a fashionable skirt with a matching tailored knit top in cool blue, added a white leather belt and slipped her feet into white high-heeled shoes. Her hair required a vigorous brushing to restore its smooth, loose style, then she added the merest touch of perfume, and was ready.

There was no sign of Raf as she emerged from her room, and she walked to the head of the staircase, paused fractionally to take in a deep breath, then she slowly descended to the ground floor.

With an increasing sense of trepidation she made her way towards the lounge, sure that she would find him there, drink in hand.

He was, looking incredibly vital in dark hip-hugging trousers and an open-necked white shirt. His attention was caught by the television screen, and her stomach performed a painful somersault as he became aware of her presence and turned to face her.

'A drink, Chelsea?' One eyebrow lifted in quizzical query, and she damned him to hell for his ability to present such a degree of implacable sophistication.

Crossing to the rosewood cabinet, he extracted a glass, added ice, and poured a small measure of brandy, then topped it with ginger ale and a dash of lime juice.

'I might have preferred something else.' Chelsea knew the words to be petty the instant they left her lips, but she had no intention of tempering them.

'Perhaps you would care to enlighten me?'

He knew very well she was simply being perverse, and to make it worse he was amused. 'White wine,' she answered sweetly, meeting his indolent gaze with remarkable clarity.

'Could you qualify that? I'd hate to select Riesling if you'd prefer Moselle or Pinot Chardonnay, a Sauternes or champagne.

'There's an excellent *vin blanc* in the bar fridge,' Chelsea revealed, undeterred, as she seated herself comfortably in one of several Swedish leather armchairs placed strategically around the large room.

Without a word Raf turned back to the cabinet, extracted the appropriate bottle and opened it, then he filled a slim crystal flute with the chilled wine and presented it to her.

'Salute.' His mockery was barely discernible, but there, none the less, and she sipped her wine in an effort to remain calm.

'Would it be too much to expect some form of explanation as to why you're here?'

His intent scrutiny was disturbing, yet she held his gaze with apparent equanimity, determined not to allow him any advantage.

'I understood you to give me an assurance that where the welfare of Houghton-Hamilton is concerned, I could count on your support.' His voice was silky-smooth, and far too dangerous for her to discount unconditionally.

'Yes. But I fail to see what that has to do with your presence in this house.'

Raf lifted his glass and considered its contents with abstract deliberation before swallowing a generous quantity; then he put the glass down on to a nearby table and thrust both hands into his trouser pockets.

'The stock market reversals have brought an element of extreme caution into the business sector, and I consider it imperative to visibly project Houghton-Hamilton's solidarity and thus negate any "raiding" rumours whispering around the Bourse.' He paused to give her a particularly assessing glance. 'At the moment, two factors give the so-called rumours some credence. Shares on the open market are being snapped up, and there's considerable concern among the shareholders as to how the firm will continue if, as is also rumoured, we were to divorce and you elected to sell your stake in

Houghton-Hamilton.'

Chelsea digested what he said and silently agreed with his reasoning. 'My loyalty to Houghton-Hamilton isn't in question.'

'Unfortunately, the shareholders are proving difficult to convince,' he informed her with a faint degree of mocking cynicism.

She took an appreciative sip of her wine, enjoying the chilled, sharp taste of the excellent vintage. 'I presume you have a solution?'

Raf spared her a long, considering look from beneath dark-fringed lashes, and appeared to choose his words with care. 'I think we should effect an apparent reconciliation.'

Her eyes widened slightly, and her lips parted to utter an immediate refusal. The glass in her hand began to shake and she carefully held it in both hands so that he wouldn't see just how badly her nerves were reacting. '*Apparent*?' Her voice unwittingly rose a fraction. 'You mean, you intend staying *here*?'

He gave a careless shrug, and his lips twisted to form a wry smile; 'It would scarcely be convincing if I were to take up residence in a hotel.

No! she longed to cry out. It would be bad enough if she had to face him at the office each day, but having him sleep under the same roof, sharing her meals, just *being here* . . . She couldn't bear it.

Yet within—how many hours of his arrival in Sydney, seven?—he had not only set the stage, but had manoeuvred all the players into position.

'Need I remind you that I have a perfectly legal right to be here?' he said smoothly.

Casting him a speculative glance beneath long-fringed lashes, Chelsea glimpsed the chilling sense of purpose evident, and barely resisted the urge to throw something at him.

'This so-called reconciliation—how long do you expect it to last?' She had to ask, attempt at least, to put a time limit on the length of his stay.

Raf regarded her steadily, his expression indolent and unrevealing. After what seemed an interminable silence, he informed her in a lazy drawl, 'As long as it takes.'

Chelsea's mind began to whirl at his implication. Mere weeks seemed illogical. Yet anything approaching *months* was totally untenable.

'I could release a statement,' she declared with a degree of asperity, 'announcing that my shareholding in Houghton is secure.'

Raf reached out for his glass and took another generous swallow, and the action drew attention to the strong column of his throat, the muscular cords banding his forearms and the breadth of his shoulders.

'Without sufficient proof to back it up, any such statement would be viewed with some scepticism as to its permanence.'

She felt haunted, the victim of a professional hunter about to manoeuvre his prey into a skilfully disguised trap. 'What if I don't agree?'

It was a punitive stand, and he knew it. 'This is a large home,' he indicated with undisguised mockery. 'I'm sure we can both live here without it proving too great a hardship. I trust you have no objection if I use Sam's study?'

Chelsea knew Sam would have approved Raf stepping into its revered portals. Just as he'd approved of their marriage. And arranged it.

Impossible to forget, difficult to forgive. Yet she'd learned to cope with the the anger inside her; even managed to understand Sam's motivation. What she'd never be able to condone was Raf's participation.

She lifted the crystal flute and sipped at its contents, taking her time, before spearing him with the type of studied speculation that had brought lesser men to their knees. 'Don't you think it's stretching credibility a bit too far for the very people you hope to convince that, after a two-year absence and with very little contact at all in that time, we've fallen madly into each other's arms and decided to set up house again?' It was incredible, but she was actually enjoying herself. 'I have—friends,' she went on with delicate emphasis, 'who take delight in despatching news clippings depicting your every move. An accurate count would provide at least thirty newsprint photographs portraying the eminent Raf Hamilton in the company of yet another, different, social beauty.' Her mouth curved faintly to form a supposedly whimsical smile. 'Why, I do believe that comes out at something like one for every three or four weeks.' She shook her head in silent remonstrance, then tilted it slightly as she held his gaze. 'One can only assume you crave variety, or alternatively, become easily bored.' She paused, then poisoned the mythical dart. 'Hardly an advertisement for sobriety, would you say? Although of course a man is easily forgiven such dalliances, whereas a woman is expected to remain chastely virtuous.'

Something flared in the depths of Raf's eyes, then they hardened, and his mouth twisted into a sardonic smile. 'Have you remained chastely virtuous, Chelsea?'

Her head slid back at his silkily voiced query, and she willingly allowed herself to become trapped in his gaze.

'You mean you don't *know*, Raf? With Jonathan in the office, and—ah, let me guess—a diligent dectective tracking my movements outside it?'

For a moment she thought she'd gone too far, for his features became granite-hard and totally implacable.

'Accept that I considered it a necessary precaution for your safety.'

'Really?' Now she'd started, she couldn't stop. 'Did you think I wouldn't eventually *notice*? Or consider that I might be scared witless at discovering I was being followed?' Resentment flared, deepening the colour of her eyes and giving them a fiery sparkle. 'You could have at least ensured that I knew!'

'Are there any other grievances you'd like to air?' His mocking query brought a surge of renewed anger.

'Several. I'll make a list.'

He lifted his glass and drained the remaining contents before setting it down on a nearby table. 'Shall we go in to dinner?' His eyes flashed with fire and Chelsea wondered at her temerity in opposing him.

'I'm not in the least hungry,' she retorted with considerable exasperation. It was nothing less than the truth, for her appetite had vanished soon after she'd entered the lounge.

'Nevertheless you will eat something. You look incredibly—delicate. Almost fragile.'

Chelsea threw him a stormy glance. 'My weight hasn't varied more than a kilo or two in years.'

Raf shortened the distance between them with lazy, catlike strides, and she resisted the instinctive need to sink further into the soft leather cushioning as he removed her empty glass, then he caught hold of her hand and drew her to her feet.

'Dinner, Chelsea.' He relinquished his hold almost at once, and she assured herself she was relieved.

Yet her fingers tingled from his touch, and she was supremely conscious of an acute awareness as she preceded him into the elegantly furnished dining-room, where, she saw at a glance, Hannah had surpassed herself in utilising the finest linen, bone china and cutlery from their considerable collection. An exquisite floral arrangement graced the table's centre, with flanking candelabra.

Candles? Hannah, how could you, Chelsea inwardly despaired as she took a seat, yet her expression was calm as she removed the lid from the first of three silver dishes to reveal a succulent beef *bourguignon*, accompanied by rice and an assortment of vegetables. Dessert comprised a fresh fruit compôte with clotted cream, and there were various cheeses beneath a glass dome. A veritable feast, yet she doubted she could eat more than a few morsels.

'No more wine,' she refused as Raf uncorked the bottle and moved to fill her glass.

'The need for a clear head?'

Why prevaricate and be a source of his amusement?

'Yes.' She gave him a bleak look, holding his mocking gaze without difficulty at all.

'I'll serve,' Raf indicated smoothly, unfolding his napkin from its elaborate design. 'If you'll pass me your plate?'

'I'd prefer to help myself.' There was no way she'd allow him the privilege of apportioning her food, knowing it would be far more than she could manage. The amount she selected looked pitifully small on her plate, and she forked the first mouthful, barely tasting the excellent beef as she viewed him circumspectly beneath lowered lashes.

His serving was generous, and she found herself wondering idly if he had supplemented her sandwich with lunch. Not that she had any intention of asking, or admitting even to herself that she cared!

The stretching silence between them began to play havoc with her nerves, and looked certain to prove disastrous where her digestion was concerned. What topic of conversation could she pursue after an absence of two years? Any mention of the weather was as trite as a query relating to his business or social life.

Damn! Yesterday—even this morning, her existence had appeared so ordered, *normal*. Now she was on edge, infinitely wary, and as tongue-tied as an adolescent schoolgirl.

'Lost for words, Chelsea?'

She gave a slight shrug as she replaced her cutlery and pushed her plate aside. 'Choose a subject of conversation, and I'll willingly pursue it.'

'How—refreshingly civilised,' drawled Raf, leaning back in his chair. 'Tell me, is that all you're going to eat?'

Any more, she acknowledged silently, and my stomach will revolt. 'Your concern is touching. Can I now expect a lecture on nutrition?'

His expression didn't alter, and after a few long seconds she glanced away, feeling cross and distinctly at odds with herself, with *him*.

'After a long transatlantic flight, and very little sleep in the past forty-eight hours, I've no inclination to begin an argument,' he reasoned.

'We seem to strike sparks off each other,' she explained with a gesture of helpless angry resignation, and felt a tinge of pink colour her cheeks at the cynical lift of his eyebrow.

'Have you ever wondered *why*?'

'Oh, yes,' she declared cynically, offering a smile that tilted the edges of her mouth and barely reached her eyes. 'It kept me awake at night, for months. Then I realised that knowing the answer didn't necessarily solve the problem.'

His eyes never left her face. 'Why not confide in me?'

For a moment Chelsea almost held her breath, and the ensuing silence became electric; then she laughed, a strangely humourless sound, as she slowly shook her head in silent negation. 'Telling you won't provide a solution.'

'That bad, Chelsea?'

The taunting softness of his query made her feel incredibly angry. She rose to her feet and placed her napkin on the table.

'In such a hurry to escape?'

'It's been quite a day, one way and another,' she

retorted, all too aware of an intense weariness that wasn't helped by the electric tension between them. 'I'm going upstairs to bed.'

'I think I'll join you.'

'Not in my bed, you won't!' The words were out before she could give them thought, and she stood there transfixed as he discarded his napkin and rose from his chair.

'Did I suggest an intention to make love to you?'

She looked at him, wildly uncertain at the silky cynicism evident, then anger resurfaced as she glimpsed his mocking amusement. 'Go to hell, Raf!'

Without a further word she walked from the room, resisting the temptation to run once she reached the stairs, and it wasn't until she was safely in her own bedroom that she allowed herself to slump against the closed door, her breathing as ragged as if she'd climbed a dozen flights, instead of merely one.

Damn him, she cursed vengefully. *Damn him*!

CHAPTER FOUR

IT SEEMED an age before Chelsea roused herself sufficiently to go through the mechanical movements of slipping out of her clothes and preparing for bed. She had progressed beyond mere tiredness to a point where she was unable to relax sufficiently to cull sleep.

How could she *sleep* with Raf occupying the same suite? A hundred different images flooded her brain in colourful kaleidoscopic confusion, and with an agonised moan she turned over and thumped the pillow in an effort to *forget*. Except that the memories returned, a taunting, intrusive force that couldn't be ignored as her imagination ran riot, vividly seeing him prepare for bed, his tautly muscled frame revealed as he divested each article of clothing.

Was he lying in bed, wide awake, tormented by her presence close by, possessed of an all too graphic recollection of their lovemaking—as *she* was?

She thumped the pillow again with a groan of disgust. If she allowed her thoughts to continue their wayward direction, she'd never get to sleep! As for Raf—he'd long since acquired the knack of being able to summon somnolence at will—an important asset for someone who travelled the world's length and breadth as frequently as he did, she conceded uncharitably.

A hollow, self-derisory laugh escaped her lips. In all probability he wasn't even in bed yet; opting instead for an after-dinner brandy in the comfort of the lounge, his mind occupied with a surplus of business details.

Half an hour later she considered delving into the recess of her medicine cabinet for a sleeping pill, knowing that if she didn't manage at least six hours' sleep she wouldn't be able to function adequately the next day.

Except that the packet was no longer there, Chelsea discovered as she rummaged through the cabinet. Remembering Hannah's penchant for checking expiry dates on all medication, she thought the pills had presumably been discarded down the waste disposal months ago. Paracetamol and hot milk would have to suffice, she decided with a degree of resignation, and, slipping her arms into a silk wrap, she left the bedroom and made her way down to the kitchen.

A dimmed light illuminated the staircase, and on reaching the lower floor she moved towards the eastern side of the house, entering the large, well-equipped kitchen only to come to a sudden halt at the sight of Raf, shirt carelessly unbuttoned, removing a steaming saucepan from the benchtop element.

He looked up the instant the door opened, and every last nerve-end tingled alive, making her shockingly aware of him.

'Unable to sleep, Chelsea?' The soft drawl matched the faint mockery evident in those dark eyes, and succeeded in provoking a sickening lurch in the region of her stomach.

What was the use of denying it? Besides, it was self-evident from the faint, almost-bruised looking smudges beneath her eyes, the pale translucence of her skin. 'Yes.'

'Care to try some hot milk, brandy, with a dash of kahlua?' He filled a glass with milk, set the empty saucepan into the sink, then raised the glass to his lips and swallowed a generous mouthful before extending the glass towards her. 'Warm, potent, and guaranteed to smooth out all the rough edges.'

Chelsea eyed him carefully, unsure whether or not to retreat. He looked incredibly dangerous—almost lethal. The elusive tang of his aftershave teased her nostrils, and the warmth of his body seemed to reach out like an electrifying magnet as she drew close.

Without a word he lifted the glass to her lips, and she sipped the contents like an obedient child, feeling the fiery warmth of spirits diluted in milk course down her throat, desensitising a profusion of jangling nerve-ends and invading her body with a curious lethargic inertia.

He held the glass firm until it was half empty, then he removed it and slowly drained the remaining contents before replacing the glass on the bench. His eyes were dark and slumbrous, and she felt trapped in their depths, aware of a treacherous weakness over which she appeared to possess little control.

With a sense of terrible fascination she watched as he lifted a hand and idly traced the fullness of her lips before letting his fingers brush across her cheek to bury themselves in the silkiness of her hair. His head lowered, and she stood mesmerised as his breath fanned her cheek, then his lips touched the corner of her mouth in a gentle caress, provocative and faintly teasing as he edged the tip of his tongue over the soft, sweet curves, tasting with a feather-lightness that made her ache for more.

Of their own volition her lips parted, unconsciously inviting his possession as her tongue sought his, instinctively cajoling, tantalising, until she sensed his soft intake of breath; then his mouth hardened as it mastered hers, demanding, in at kiss that was totally devastating.

Somehow her arms crept up to clasp behind his neck as she unwittingly moved close against him, and her whole body became vibrantly alive as his hand slid down to capture her breast.

There was a wealth of seduction in his touch, and an inaudible moan of self-defeat escaped her lips as his mouth trailed down the sensitive cord of her neck and tasted the hollows at the base of her throat before travelling lower to savour the delicate peak that burgeoned in welcome of his possession.

A slow ache manifested itself in the region of her stomach, and spread steadily until she became utterly mindless, aware of a strange floating sensation as Raf placed an arm beneath her knees and lifted her high against his chest to carry her with effortless ease towards the staircase.

She was aware of burying her face against his neck, the soft, husky chuckle sounding deep in his throat as he reached his room, then she was being lowered down to stand before him, and as his hand reached for the remaining buttons on his shirt the enormity of what was about to happen assailed her with frightening clarity, and she wrenched away from him, filled with sickening despair. 'No—*no*!'

For a moment he went curiously still. 'Up until a few seconds ago, you were giving me a definite *yes*,' Raf drawled cynically.

Suddenly Chelsea had great difficulty in swallowing, and it took an immense effort to meet and hold his gaze. His eyes narrowed fractionally, and she sensed the latent anger beneath the surface of his control.

She felt tortured, and most damning of all— betrayed.

'I could make you crave my possession until you *begged* for release,' he threatened softly. In the shadowed half-light reflected from a nearby wall sconce he appeared large and formidable, and she didn't have time to cry out as his mouth closed over hers in a kiss that was as shattering to her equilibrium as he'd intended.

When at last he lifted his head, silly, stupid tears welled up behind her lids and seeped through to trickle slowly down each cheek until they came to rest at the edge of her chin.

If Raf had wanted to punish her, he'd succeeded, she decided numbly as she let her hands fall to her sides. Not once had he ever kissed her with quite that degree of plundering savagery, nor subjected her to such ravaging retribution.

'For goodness' sake, go to bed,' Raf directed hardily, his eyes dark and inscrutable. 'Or I'll put you in mine, and damn the consequences!'

There wasn't an ounce of remorse evident, and she stood transfixed, frozen into agonising silence, where words—anything she might possibly use in retaliation, seemed locked in her brain. Yet somehow she managed to dredge up sufficient impetus to turn away from him and walk towards the connecting door, incapable of doing anything but close it quietly behind her before crossing the sitting-room to her own bedroom.

Her movements were akin to those of an automaton, and in the relative safety of her room she abstractedly straightened the twisted sheets, then slid into bed. The desire to weep was uppermost, but no tears would come, and she lay still, too emotionally drained to do anything but close her eyes and pray that sheer exhaustion would soon provide a much-needed escape into merciful oblivion.

Chelsea must have slept, for she woke to discover bright sunshine filtering through the edges of her bedroom curtains. Too much sunshine, she determined upon glancing at her bedside clock, for it was well after eight, and even if she showered and dressed in record time there was not the remotest chance she could reach the office before nine o'clock.

Even so, she attempted the impossible, and went into the kitchen to collect a glass of fresh orange juice from the refrigerator, surprising Hannah, who was in the process of loading the dishwater.

'I haven't time for anything else,' she said after extending an initial greeting. 'I overslept.'

Hannah straightened from her task and looked faintly perplexed. 'I assumed you weren't going into the office. Raf left instructions for you not to be disturbed.'

Had he, indeed? That was presumptuous of him, to say the least, Chelsea derided silently as she poured juice, then hurriedly drained the glass. Rather than compound the situation, she elected silence and an over-bright smile. Placing the empty glass on the bench, she plucked a tissue from its container nearby and carefully blotted her lipstick.

'I must dash. I'll see you tonight.'

Hannah's frown deepened. 'Raf said you'd both be dining out.'

He had? Aloud, Chelsea managed a light laugh, and followed it with, 'Of course, how could I have forgotten?'

On going into the garage, she noticed at once that Raf's Jaguar was missing, and she slid into her Porsche, fired the engine and sent the car growling down the driveway, inclined in a moment of sheer rage to indulge in a burst of unmitigated speed with wheels spinning and the sound of squealing tyres.

But caution overruled recklessness, and she deliberately set a sedate pace, negotiating the traffic with ease to reach the offices of Houghton-Hamilton just prior to nine-thirty.

'I didn't expect to see you today,' Susan remarked with surprise as Chelsea swept past her secretary's desk, and it took considerable effort to summon a semblance of normality.

'I overslept,' Chelsea explained, aware as soon as the words emerged that she was fuelling the office grapevine with conjecture.

'Mr Hamilton rang through an hour ago to say that you probably wouldn't be in today.'

She discerned Susan's curiosity, and deliberately strove for an expression of bland inscrutability. 'As you can see, I changed my mind.'

That was another count against Raf, and it appeared

she might have to keep score—one she eventually intended to settle, she decided darkly as she continued into her office, discovering at once the two daily newspapers placed discreetly on top of her desk—open at page three, where a wedding photo riveted her attention. Familiar, because it was her own, and her eyes rapidly scanned the caption, widening considerably and filling with expressive anger as she read that Chelsea and Raf Hamilton had effected a reconciliation after a two-year separation.

There was no doubt who was responsible for instigating the news-media attention, she decided furiously, as she reached for the telephone and punched out the requisite number of buttons to connect her with Jonathan's office.

'It's Chelsea, Jonathan. I don't suppose Raf is with you, is he?' she queried, outwardly calm, whereas inwardly she was positively seething.

'Good morning,' her husband's right-hand man acknowledged with a tinge of humour. 'No. However, you can reach him on the extension in the front office.'

Chelsea gritted her teeth, thanked him, then pressed down the handset, released it and punched out a new set of numbers.

'Hamilton,' Raf answered almost immediately, his voice sounding compellingly vital from the other end of the line.

Chelsea's stomach gave a painful lurch, and her knuckles whitened as she clutched the receiver. 'Perhaps you'd care to explain precisely what right you have to print that article in today's newspapers?' she began without preamble. 'And informing Susan I wouldn't be in today.' Anger engulfed her, deepening her voice and making her breath come in short sharp bursts. 'And telling Hannah we won't be in for dinner!' She was so incensed, she felt as if she was about to explode.

'Rather than invite speculative conjecture about my reappearance in Sydney and the state of our relationship, I opted for a formal announcement. A celebratory dinner seemed a natural progression,' Raf drawled. 'And you appeared so deeply asleep when I checked on you early this morning that I told Hannah to leave you undisturbed.'

'What do you mean, when you checked on me?' Her voice rose almost an octave, and she just prevented herself from shouting. 'How *dare* you? As to dinner—you can go out on your own. I'm certainly not joining you!' She slammed down the handset before he had the opportunity to reply.

Seconds later she picked up her pen, determined to attend to some paperwork, only to discover her hand was shaking so badly that she could barely write.

Damn, *damn*! *Why* did he have to come back and disrupt her life all over again? Worse, why had she permitted herself to be manoeuvred into such an invidious position? It was a one-way street, where the only way out was to go on. But how far, and for how long? Even more pertinent was, could she survive with her emotions intact?

She lifted a shaky hand and combed her fingers through the length of her hair, her eyes becoming pensive with introspection. After last night, there was little doubt her body was its own traitorous mistress. Lust, she assured herself with self-deprecatory disgust. *Lust*, a simple craving of the flesh, nothing more.

Yet, if that were true, why hadn't she been sufficiently fascinated by other men during the past two years? Heaven knew, several had tried very hard to infiltrate her cool exterior. Some had even referred to her frigidity. That was a laugh! With Raf she was like a nubile wanton, only too willing to taste every sensual pursuit and return it twofold. The knowledge made her feel faintly ill.

With a gesture of futility she replaced her pen, then stood and paced a path round her desk in an effort to channel her thoughts away from her dynamic husband. Work, she determined stoically, was supposed to be a panacea for all ills. All it required was dedicated application.

And work she did—all day, without so much as a break for a lunch, having Susan send out for sandwiches, and declining all but essentially important phone calls. Consequently, by five o'clock she was exhausted, in a manner that left her bone-weary but pleasantly self-satisfied with her own achievement.

With a deep sigh she flexed her shoulders and slowly eased back in her chair as Susan collected a sheaf of completed papers from the desk.

'I won't say a word,' her secretary murmured with an admonishing shake of her head, and Chelsea gave her a faint smile.

'Don't.'

'Except—go home,' Susan advised gently. 'You look dead-beat.'

Chelsea stood to her feet and caught up her

briefcase, along with her bag. 'I intend to. Goodnight, and thanks,' she added quietly, meeting the sympathetic warmth in Susan's eyes. 'I'll see you tomorrow.'

'Monday,' the other woman corrected. 'It's the weekend, remember?'

Chelsea momentarily closed her eyes. 'Christmas,' she offered with a shrug. 'I've lost track of the days.'

Somehow she had expected Raf to make some kind of contact during the day. If not in person, at least by phone. The fact that he had done neither was vaguely disturbing, and she frowned as she watched Susan leave. A tiny grimace made a fleeting appearance on her expressive features. Perhaps she was a fool to even attempt to flout Raf. Yet, no matter how plausible his explanation, she was damned if she'd meekly comply with every single arrangement he made.

The desire to linger temporarily confused her, until she realised she didn't really want to go home. No, that wasn't strictly true, she mused distractedly. She wanted to avoid seeing Raf and evade the tension he was able to evoke. Yet there was no escape. He had personally made sure of it, and she hated being caught up in his subterfuge, aware of its necessity, yet an unwilling participant.

'Finished for the day?'

Chelsea glanced up at the sound of that deep drawl, and met those dark eyes with fearless disregard. 'Yes. I was just about to leave.'

Raf subjected her to a swift, raking appraisal, which she bore with unblinking composure. 'Likewise. I suggest we depart together.'

Without a further word she preceded him from her office, and suffered his light clasp of her elbow as they stood waiting for the elevator. In the confined space of the electronic cubicle she stood in silence, aware of the veiled interest they engendered, and locked into the indisputable aura of power Raf managed to exude. Something most men coveted, but few managed to achieve, she decided idly. Women found him incredibly fascinating, drawn as if by a magnet to his potent brand of sexual chemistry. A composite which was infinitely dangerous to anyone's peace of mind—especially *hers*.

Within seconds of reaching the basement car park, she decided she must be hallucinating. Her Porsche wasn't in its parking bay, nor, she ascertained with a quick encompassing glance, was it anywhere in sight.

'What have you done with my car?'

'Had it driven home, courtesy of an eager young clerk who thought all his birthdays had come at once,' Raf told her with ill-concealed mockery. 'The Jaguar is over there.'

The fingers clasping her elbow held the threat of steel if she dared to pull free. 'You honestly expect me to docilely conform?'

'Docility would be advisable.' His smile was a mere facsimile, and for some unknown reason Chelsea had the instinctive sensation he was biding time for the right moment to pounce. There was a stalking quality apparent in his manner which she found distinctly unnerving.

'You'll take me home?'

'After we've eaten—yes,' he agreed with silky detachment. 'And don't argue,' he added with dangerous softness. 'Hannah reported that you left without breakfast, and Susan, when pressed, admitted she sent out for sandwiches at lunch, half of which you returned uneaten.

Traitors, both of them, Chelsea decided as Raf led her towards the powerful-looking car.

Within minutes the Jaguar reached the exit and was purring smoothly along the streets beneath Raf's expert handling. Chelsea sank back against the handcrafted leather seat and let her head rest comfortably as she centred her attention beyond the windscreen.

The traffic was heavy, and there were the usual delays at various intersections, making progress relatively slow.

'Where are you taking me?' she felt inclined to query, adding, 'Or daren't I ask?'

He spared her a swift glance, his expression infinitely cynical. 'Double Bay,' he informed her drily, and she made a faint *moue*.

'I'm not exactly dressed for it, and my make-up is almost non-existent.'

His attention didn't waver from the road. 'I'm sure you carry a powder compact and lipstick—sufficient for running repairs.'

Chelsea refrained from answering, and minutes later the car slid in to the kerb. For a moment she considered remaining obstinate, then common sense prevailed.

Raf turned his head slightly and watched the flicker of emotions chase across her expressive features. 'Shall we go?'

Chelsea lifted her chin and met his cool, enigmatic

gaze. 'Has no other woman told you that barbarism died with the Dark Ages?'

A faint smile lurked in the depths of his dark eyes and his mouth curved with wry humour. 'My dear Chelsea—*barbarism*? I would hope to employ a far more subtle approach than dragging you by the hair into my lair.'

'There's nothing subtle about invading my life, announcing a supposed reconciliation without my consent, and forcing me to share a meal with you that I distinctly remembering refusing,' she declared evenly in an effort to flout him.

'Are we going to sit here and bandy words all night?' There was a hint of steel apparent, and with a slight shrug she unclipped her seat-belt and slid from the car, waiting on the pavement as Raf locked up.

The restaurant was small and intimate, yet undoubtedly one of the expensively élite dining establishments the city had to offer, and it soon became apparent that recognition guaranteed deferential service—from the extremely expensive champagne offered, and the *maître d's* almost obsequious assurance that the chef would prepare anything of their choice, even if it was not shown on the menu.

'Will you permit me to order for you?'

Chelsea sipped the excellent champagne and directed Raf a clear, considering glance across the rim of her fluted glass. Already the potent bubbles were exploding inside her stomach and reaching deep into the centre of her nervous system, calming all the frayed edges and filling her with a delicious relaxing warmth.

'Providing it's something light in texture and quantity,' she returned evenly.

'Perhaps I should take advantage of such complicity,' Raf murmured drily. 'It may never happen again.'

Chelsea met his dark, enigmatic gaze with equanimity. 'You make me sound like a recalcitrant child!'

His mouth relaxed to form a humorous smile. 'Hardly a child, Chelsea. Yet you derive a certain satisfaction out of thwarting me—often for the sheer hell of it, I suspect.'

'Has it never occurred to you that I might be deliberately providing variety from the thousands of women who fawn all over your handsome body and become enthralled with your every word?'

She saw one eyebrow lift in quizzical query. '*Thousands*?'

'Oh, *yes*. I refuse to believe you're unaware of the effect you have on the opposite sex.' Her eyes took on a mysterious depth as her lips curved to form a winsome smile. 'During our brief marriage, at least two threatened my demise, several promised me physical harm, and one host assured me it was only Sam's money and entrée into a business partnership that precipitated our ill-fated alliance.'

'We still are,' Raf offered cynically, and her eyes widened in momentary incomprehension. 'Married,' he spelled out patiently.

'I imagine you find it suitably convenient to have a wife in the background, providing an escape route whenever a relationship becomes too——' She paused delicately. 'Difficult.'

'You think I'm incapable of keeping those *thousands* of women at bay?' Raf sounded lightly amused, but she detected a thread of steel beneath the surface, almost anger, and a slight shiver slithered its way down the length of her spine.

'Only those you want to,' she managed with outward composure, infinitely relieved when the waiter appeared out of nowhere and consulted at great length with Raf over the choice of sauces that should accompany each selection of dishes.

Chelsea sipped her champagne and let her gaze wander slowly round the room, noting with interest that several patrons had elected to grace the establishment, despite the relatively early hour.

Discovering her glass was empty, she put it down on to the table, letting her finger idly trace the flute's base before seeking the delicate convolutions on its stem.

'More champagne?'

She glanced up and met Raf's dark, inscrutable gaze with considerable calm as she silently acquiesced, aware of a delicious floaty sensation that had the vague effect of slowing her reflexes. Perhaps she shouldn't have any more champagne until she'd eaten something, she decided, watching the aerated bubbles with detached interest.

'Have you arranged for a Press photographer to appear and record this moment for posterity, as well as providing tangible proof for the stockholders?'

'Not deliberately,' Raf drawled. 'Although we each are sufficiently well known to attract interest, and after appearing in newsprint this morning I imagine any newshound worth his salt will jump at the opportunity to collect a scoop—*if* one happens to discover our presence here.'

The starter was presented with the flourish it deserved, and Chelsea spread croutons into the aromatic chicken consommé, slowly spooning every mouthful until the plate was empty.

Next came a delicious home-made pasta in a delicate creamy-cheese sauce with mushrooms, accompanied by crisp fingers of garlic-buttered toast. Heaven, she decided, and wondered how Raf had discovered this gourmet's delight of a restaurant.

'Jonathan awarded it his highest recommendation,' Raf explained, and she cast him a startled look, unsure whether she had voiced the query aloud. Then she caught the faint mockery evident and knew he'd managed to read her mind—a fact which had often unnerved her in the past, for it made her feel distinctly uncomfortable to have someone so acutely aware of her thoughts, almost as if they held licence to see into her soul.

The main course proved to be roast saddle of lamb à *l'arlésienne*, served with a garnish of new potatoes, mushrooms and truffles.

Chelsea refused more than a mere morsel of each, and forked small mouthfuls of the delectable food, silently pacing herself to finish simultaneously with Raf.

For something to do she absently sipped her champagne, aware of an elusive alchemy that melted her bones and played havoc with her equilibrium.

'What thoughts are whirling inside your head?'

The query, so silkily soft, took her unwares, and

she answered without thinking. 'Memories.'

'Would you care to elucidate?'

If she said *us*, you and me, three years ago, when I thought I was in love . . . A silent sadness rose like a lump in her throat, and she swallowed to disperse it, managing with practised panache to force a light laugh. 'Sam, boarding-school, my year in Switzerland. When life was relatively carefree and uncomplicated.' Amazing, but she was even able to meet Raf's hooded gaze.

Dessert was presented in the form of a strawberry flan Chantilly, and proved to be utterly delicious.

'Coffee? Irish, Jamaican?'

Chelsea hesitated only briefly, unsure whether more alcohol in any quantity was wise. 'Jamaican.'

She sipped it appreciatively when it came, savouring the smooth, spicy taste with enjoyment, and watched as Raf finished his Irish coffee before he signalled for the bill, signed it and pocketed the duplicate.

There was no reason to linger, and she preceded him out on to the pavement where a number of people were window-shopping, taking advantage of the longer hours of daylight and merely strolling to enjoy the cooler evening air after the day's stultifying heat.

'What would you like to do now?'

For some reason she was strangely reluctant to return home, and she turned towards him with a poignantly wistful smile. 'Walk barefoot along the beach.'

Raf cast her a look that held veiled cynicism. 'We're not exactly dressed for it.'

Her smile deepened, forming irrepressible dimples in each cheek. 'You could roll up your trousers, loosen your tie.'

'Are you challenging me?'

Her smile faltered and her expression slowly sobered. 'No. I could never win.'

'So sure, Chelsea?'

There was no room for indecision. 'Yes.'

'Lead the way to the beach,' Raf directed, and without a word she walked down towards the sandy foreshore where, once there, she slipped off her shoes.

There was a soft breeze coming off the sea, and the water looked infinitely cool and inviting. Children in the distance raced and played, their laughter shrill with pleasure, joining the keening cries of soaring gulls that coasted down to peck at titbits of food.

It was a simple scene, and Chelsea lifted her face slightly to catch the breeze, letting it tease the tendrils of her hair, cooling her skin.

She sensed rather than heard Raf come up beside her, and cast him a quick sideways glance, discovering that he had his jacket hooked over one shoulder and his elegant, handcrafted shoes tucked under one arm.

They walked in companionable silence, stopping occasionally as Raf collected shells and skimmed them out on to the gleaming surface of the sea. By the time they reached the end of the cove dusk had begun to descend, and they turned and unhurriedly began to retrace their steps.

Chelsea stumbled once and his arm curved round her waist, steadying her. His clasp was light and in no way binding, yet she was supremely conscious of every breath she took, every step. This close, she could smell the faint muskiness of his skin mingling with his cologne, and she was so intensely aware of him that she ached to be held, kissed, *loved*—slowly, and with such incredible gentleness that the loving and its aftermath would last most of the night. As it had in the beginning. Yet one could never go back, she reflected sadly. There was only *now*.

'It might be a good idea to arrange a party early next week, invite a few friends, business associates.'

Chelsea blinked, discarding her wayward thoughts in an effort to deal with the present. 'Which particular evening do you have in mind?' she queried slowly, feeling oddly reluctant to re-enter the social circuit, yet aware that it would be expected in light of their publicised reconciliation.

'Tuesday? That should provide Hannah with sufficient notice to organise the catering.'

It was almost dark, the evening light fading rapidly once the sun slipped beyond the horizon, and she shivered slightly.

'Cold?'

She shook her head in silent negation. 'No.' How could she explain how difficult it would be for her to attempt to shine and present a happy, contented image when inside she knew it to be merely a façade? Aware that together they would be the cynosure of all eyes, half of which would be feminine and only too anxious to study her every move, waiting, watching for the slightest crack to appear in her chosen mask.

'Afraid?'

For a stark moment the breath caught in her throat.

'Should I be?' she countered lightly. 'I graduated from a highly reputable finishing-school proficient in teaching all the social graces. 'I'm sure I can manage to gaze at you in seeming adoration whenever we're in company.'

'And revert to a pocket spitfire whenever we're alone,' Raf drawled imperturbably.

'Probably,' Chelsea responded steadily, unwilling to let him see the slightest chink in her armour. They reached the street's entrance and walked towards the car, where she waited while Raf unlocked her door before slipping into the passenger seat.

She didn't offer so much as a word during the drive home. Not that it mattered, for he simply inserted a tape into the cassette deck and music provided a soothing background of sound that precluded the need for conversation.

It was after nine when Raf turned into the driveway, and once inside the house she made straight for the stairs, intending to shower and go to bed.

'A nightcap, Chelsea?'

She turned to face him, unable to discern anything from his expression. 'No, I'm really very tired.' Good manners made her add, 'Thanks for an enjoyable meal.'

A slow smile tugged the edge of his mouth. 'So—thank me.'

A prickle of apprehension made itself felt in the pit of her stomach. 'I just did.'

An eyebrow slanted with deliberate mockery. 'I'm sure you can do better than that.'

She looked at him in disbelief, her eyes sparkling a

brilliant fiery green. 'Oh, no, Raf, I'm not about to fall into that trap.'

'Pity,' he drawled, lifting a hand to tuck a few stray tendrils of hair behind her ear, allowing his fingers to linger against the sensitive cord of her neck. 'Goodnight, *querida*,' he taunted softly. 'Sleep well.'

Her eyes widened fractionally, then became filled with haunting heartache at that Spanish endearment, for it brought back a flood of memories too painful to endure.

Without a further word she turned and ran up the stairs, only slowing slightly when she reached the wide passageway that led to her bedroom.

Damn his teasing arrogance! she cursed. Just once she'd like to see him reduced to a state of vulnerability—to feel as acutely sensitive as he was able to make her feel.

A shower eased some of her inner tension, and, her toilette completed, she slipped into a slither of silk that served as nightwear and slid into bed, to lie gazing at the patterns of light reflected against the opposite wall until sleep provided a merciful oblivion.

CHAPTER FIVE

SATURDAY dawned bright and clear, a typical summer's day with the promise of high temperatures—ideal for a sojourn at any one of several beaches dotting the many coves and inlets that comprised this sprawling metropolis, Chelsea decided over her solitary breakfast. Raf, Hannah told her, had already eaten and was entrenched in the study, where he had been since the very early hours. Chelsea wondered uncharitably if his pre-dawn contact with the States related to business or pleasure.

Not that she cared, she assured herself as she changed into a bikini and covered it with a skirt and top. Gathering up a beach towel, sunglasses and other requisites necessary for sunbathing, she ran lightly downstairs to the kitchen.

'I'll be back late this afternoon.'

'It's the Mathysens' party tonight. Eight o'clock,' Hannah reminded her as she closed a portable cold-pack and held it out. 'I've prepared something for your lunch, and there's a container of juice in there.'

Chelsea leant forward and placed a kiss against the older woman's cheek. 'Thanks, you're a darling.'

The Porsche eased its way steadily north to Clareville beach, a lovely sequestered stretch where she could sunbathe and read in relative seclusion.

On reflection it was a wonderfully relaxed day, the sun's rays extremely warm, gilding her honey-gold skin with a deeper glow which was carefully monitored with frequent applications of sunscreen cream.

It was so peaceful, she was oddly reluctant to leave, and she looked at the water longingly for several minutes before opting to delay her swim until she reached home. At this time of year sharks were known to inhabit the coastal waters, and there was no sense in taking unnecessary risk.

Packing everything into the car, she slipped in behind the wheel and drove at a sedate pace, her mind partially occupied with what she would wear to the Mathysens' mentally sifting through her wardrobe selecting and discarding a variety of suitable dresses.

Such preoccupations lasted until she reached home, and after garaging the Porsche she deposited the portable cold-pack in the kitchen, then she slipped out of the side door and made her way towards the patio at the rear of the house.

The pool looked inviting, its blue-tiled depths giving the water a sparkling clarity, and discarding her sunglasses she executed a neat dive and surfaced midway to stroke several vigorous lengths before turning on to her back to drift aimlessly, her eyes closed against the late afternoon sun.

'Do you intend staying there much longer?'

Chelsea's eyes flew open at the sound of Raf's deep drawl, and she turned her head slightly to see his broad frame outlined against the white-painted wrought-iron gazebo nearby.

Perhaps it was a sense of self-preservation that prompted her to execute sufficient side-strokes to bring her to the pool's edge. Not that he wasn't familiar with her body, but she doubted her ability to continue lying there with any degree of composure beneath his deliberate appraisal.

'I was just about to get out,' she said coolly as she lifted a hand to smooth excess water from her hair.

Raf looked almost indecently attractive clothed in shorts and a cream, casual, open-necked shirt that accented his natural athlete's body. His eyes filled with mocking amusement as he leant forward and collected her towel from where it lay draped across a chair. 'You have half an hour in which to shower and change,' he informed her indolently as he moved towards her and extended his hand.

Chelsea ignored it and stayed exactly where she was. 'I have an invitation to Bryce Mathysen's party, which starts at eight. It doesn't take me two hours to get ready.'

'Bryce rang shortly after you left, expressing his delight at our togetherness, and insisted we join him and Alyse for dinner.' His eyes assumed an inflexible quality. 'Alyse was most voluble in her assurance that it was absolutely no bother at all.'

'What if I said I'd prefer to give dinner a miss?'

'That would make things awkward when I've already accepted.'

Her eyes became stormy. 'Something you had absolutely no right to do!'

'On the contrary,' Raf declared with a thread of amusement in his voice. 'You weren't here to ask, and it seemed churlish to refuse. Now get out, there's a good girl.'

To be treated like a spoilt *child* was the living end. 'And if I don't?'

His eyes became faintly hooded, and his voice held the silky threat of deadly intent. 'I can promise you won't like the consequences.'

Chelsea suppressed a shiver, and knew it had absolutely nothing to do with being cold. Perhaps it would be advisable to capitulate—for now. Raf had the sheer strength to physically remove her from the pool, and public dignity was something she strove at all costs to preserve. In a small gesture of defiance she swam to the shallow end and emerged via the sweep of tiled steps, realising too late that he held her towel, leaving her little alternative but to walk to where he stood.

She was supremely conscious of her scanty attire, and a dull flush coloured her cheeks at his brooding appraisal. He made her feel—exposed, she decided with raw animosity. Naked, a tiny voice taunted. Three years ago she would have smiled, tempting with warm provocativeness, accepting his kiss, and glorying in the promise of being in his arms. Now she simply held her hand for the towel and wrapped it round her slim curves with more haste than care, and he *knew*. She could read it in his eyes, sense it from the faint mockery evident in his gaze.

Without a word she brushed past him and moved quickly indoors, ascending the stairs to her suite where she stripped and showered, lathering her skin, her hair, with unnecesary vigour in an attempt to dispel the wayward tingling that coursed through her veins, distrupting her thoughts and raising such anger that it was a wonder she didn't explode with it!

Twenty-five minutes later she was ready, her make-up perfect and her hair blowdried into its familiar smooth style. Selecting what to wear took a mere few seconds, as she discarded her original choice and opted for a vibrant, multi-patterned polyester silk that shrieked its distinctive designer label.

'Ready?'

Chelsea glanced up and met Raf's assessing inspection via his mirrored reflection, and felt a renewed surge of anger. As always his tailoring was impeccable, the white fine-pleated dress-shirt accentuating his dark, attractive features and highlighting the muscular strength of his body. 'You could at least have knocked!'

Whatever for?'

He was amused, and she spun round to face him, eyes blazing. 'I value my privacy. Is it too much to expect you to do the same?'

His eyelids lowered fractionally. 'You didn't consider mine the evening I arrived,' he returned with ill-concealed mockery, and her forehead creased into an angry frown. 'While I was in the shower, you came into my room.'

It was a statement that caught her unawares, and she was left foundering for words. 'Your perfume,' he enlightened her drily. 'I also heard the click of the door as you closed it behind you—a door I had opened ten minutes previously.'

'I expected to find you unpacking,' she retorted. 'As soon as I realised you were in the shower, I left.'

'Pity,' he drawled. 'You could have joined me.'

NOW THAT THE DOOR IS OPEN...
Peel off the bouquet and send it on the postpaid order card to receive:

4 FREE BOOKS
from

An attractive 20k gold electroplated chain FREE!
And a mystery gift as an EXTRA BONUS!

PLUS

FREE HOME DELIVERY!
Once you receive your 4 FREE books and gifts, you'll be able to open your door to more great romance reading month after month. Enjoy the convenience of previewing 8 brand-new books every month delivered right to your home months before they appear in stores. Each book is yours for the low members only price of $2.24* — that's 26 cents off the retail cover price — with no additional charges for home delivery.

SPECIAL EXTRAS — FREE!
You'll also receive the "Heart to Heart" Newsletter FREE with every book shipment. Every issue is filled with interviews, news about upcoming books and more! And as a valued reader, we'll be sending you additional free gifts from time to time — as a token of our appreciation.

NO-RISK GUARANTEE!
- There's no obligation to buy — and the free books and gifts are yours to keep forever.
- You pay the low members' only price and receive books months before they appear in stores.
- You may cancel at any time, for any reason, just by sending us a note or a shipping statement marked "cancel" or by returning any shipment of books to us at our cost. Either way the free books and gifts are yours to keep!

RETURN THE POSTPAID ORDER CARD TODAY AND OPEN YOUR DOOR TO THESE 4 EXCITING LOVE-FILLED NOVELS. THEY ARE YOURS ABSOLUTELY FREE ALONG WITH YOUR 20k GOLD ELECTROPLATED CHAIN AND MYSTERY GIFT.

*Terms and prices subject to change without notice.
Sales tax applicable in NY and Iowa.
© 1989 Harlequin Enterprises Ltd.

HARLEQUIN READER SERVICE
901 FUHRMANN BLVD
PO BOX 1867
BUFFALO NY 14240-9952

Place the Bouquet here →

PLACE THE BOUQUET ON THIS CARD. FILL IT OUT AND MAIL TODAY!

Yes! I have attached the bouquet above. Please rush me my four Harlequin PRESENTS® novels along with my FREE 20k Electroplated Gold Chain and mystery gift as explained on the opposite page. I understand that accepting these books and gifts places me under no obligation ever to buy any books. I may cancel at any time for any reason, and the free books and gifts will be mine to keep!   108 CIH CAPJ (U-H-P-02/90)

Name _____

Address _____ Apt. _____

City _____ State _____

Zip _____

Take this beautiful
20k GOLD
ELECTROPLATED CHAIN
with your 4 FREE BOOKS
PLUS A MYSTERY GIFT
If offer card is missing, write to: Harlequin Reader Service,
901 Fuhrmann Blvd., P.O. Box 1867, Buffalo, NY 14269-1867.

'As if I would!'

'You used to,' he responded steadily, and she was unable to prevent the tide of colour that swept over her cheeks.

How dared he remind her? 'That was a long time ago, when I was young and foolish and *blind*.'

Raf regarded her with an unwavering scrutiny, then drawled cryptically, 'In that respect, nothing has changed.'

Chelsea became so incensed, she could have hit him, and she was conscious of her hands balling into impotent fists as she fought for some measure of control. If she didn't, this scene could rapidly descend into a slanging match. 'Shall we leave?' she queried coolly, and glimpsed his mocking smile.

'Of course. We don't want to be late.'

Without a further word she collected her evening purse from the top of her dressing-table, then preceded him from the room, the *house*, feeling anything but calm, and not looking forward at all to the evening ahead.

Alyse and Bryce Mathysen lived nearby in the prestige suburb of Seaforth, and during the ten minutes it took to reach their modern architect-designed home Chelsea elected to remain stoically silent, sure that if she did speak she would resort to the type of sarcasm she normally despised.

As Raf brought the Jaguar to a halt in the Mathysens' curved driveway, he leaned forward and switched off the ignition, then turned slightly towards her, his expression hard and inflexible.

'Need I remind you how essential it is for us to present a united front?'

She looked towards him, her gaze remarkably level. 'Oh, don't worry, Raf. I happen to regard the welfare of Houghton-Hamilton almost as highly as you do. 'My—er—*performance*,' she stressed delicately, 'will be without fault.'

'Then smile, sweetheart,' he commanded silkily. 'Alyse is about to descend.'

Chelsea glanced out of the windscreen, and there was Alyse, a vision of sheer loveliness in stark black and white, moving graciously down the steps, closely followed by a tall, silver-haired man, to greet them.

Releasing the door-clasp, she slid from the car and began walking towards their hosts, conscious of Raf close by her side.

'Darling, it's so good to see you!'

Chelsea bore Alyse's exuberant greeting, and flashed Bryce a brilliant smile as his wife slipped her arm through Raf's and guided him into the house ahead of them, chatting with a vivacious fervour that was uncontrived.

And Raf, damn him, was openly receptive, his smile warm, indolent, and totally charming. So charming, she could have kicked him, Chelsea thought dourly as she appeared to give her entire attention to Bryce's conversational platitudes as they followed Alyse and Raf indoors.

Drinks were served in the elegantly appointed lounge, and Chelsea suffered the lazy intimacy evident in Raf's gaze, managing by comparison to direct him an absolutely stunning smile at frequent intervals, feeling very much as if they were actors on a stage, playing at life.

Somehow she was able to get through the three

impeccably presented courses that comprised dinner, conscious of Alyse's subtle coquetry and Raf's bland urbanity, aware that it was a harmless little game Alyse played with any attractive man, yet the flirtatious teasing bothered her more than she cared to admit.

'Shall we adjourn to the lounge? The first of our guests should be arriving soon,' suggested Bryce, and Alyse cast her exquisite diamond-encrusted watch a casual glance.

'Good heavens, I would never have believed time could fly so quickly,' she declared breathlessly. 'Thank you, darling, for reminding me. Constance will be fraught with agitation, waiting to clear this room.' Her appealing glance encompassed them all. 'We haven't even had coffee!'

'I don't feel like coffee, do you, darling?' said Raf, and Chelsea felt her eyes widen slightly at the casually voiced endearment before she gathered herself together sufficiently to give a warm refusal.

'No, don't bother on our account, Alyse.' Just for a brief moment she glimpsed the uncertainty in the older woman's features and knew why men pampered her every wish, for Alyse was a beautiful petite doll who needed approval, and successful dinners, parties, were her lifeblood, the one thing at which she really excelled. Chelsea knew that was why Raf had agreed to dinner, because a refusal would have hurt Alyse immeasurably. 'It was a beautiful meal,' she added gently. 'And so sweet of you to insist we share it.'

'Yet you hardly ate a thing,' Alyse protested anxiously as they moved towards the lounge, and

Chelsea had to steel herself from visibly flinching as Raf placed a casual arm about her waist.

'I've already taken her to task, Alyse,' he drawled, and Chelsea momentarily closed her eyes against his intent regard, afraid to meet his gaze for fear he might define the degree of anger apparent beneath the surface of her control.

'I don't get sufficient sleep,' she ventured with a mischievous smile. 'Too many late nights and early mornings.' There, let them make of that what they liked!

'Never mind, darling,' consoled Raf as he leaned forward to brush his lips against the delicate pulsing cord at the edge of her neck. 'You have my permission to stay in bed all day and all night when we take a break in the New Year.' His eyes became lazy with promised intimacy. 'In fact, I shall insist on it.'

'Oh, I'm so *glad* the two of you have got back together,' Alyse declared, an incurable romantic at heart. 'You're perfect for each other. I've always said so, haven't I, Bryce?'

'Indeed you have,' her husband replied with an unabashed grin, which subsided slightly as chimes sounded from the vicinity of the front lobby. 'Ah, the first of our guests have arrived.' He held out his hand. 'Shall we, my dear?'

After that it was strictly smile-time as guests began to arrive, soon swelling in number to about fifty, Chelsea judged, within the span of half an hour. Most of them were mutual acquaintances, some of whom she'd known for years as friends of her father, others she'd met briefly at one function or another.

'Chelsea, *dushenka*, how wonderful to see you!'

She turned at once, her smile genuinely warm at the sound of that familiar accented voice. 'Dom—I don't believe it! What are you doing here?'

His warm features creased into a broad grin. 'You mean here in Australia, or here at his party?'

'Both,' she answered promptly, and his grin widened even further.

'Krysia wanted to come to Sydney, and I have business here,' he told her with an eloquent shrug. 'So we boarded a plane. I fly back on Tuesday, Krysia will stay a few extra days. We hope to spend Christmas together.' He glanced across the room and laughed. 'There she is now, talking to Raf.'

The last time Chelsea had seen Dom's daughter, she'd been a sixteen-year-old schoolgirl with orthodontal braces and an abundance of puppy fat. However, the girl deep in animated conversation with Chelsea's husband had undergone a startling transformation. Tall, sylph-like, and expensively dressed, she was a *femme fatale* wearing youthful confidence like a mantle. In fact, she radiated self-assurance, and clearly revelled in her role as temptress.

'Shall we join them?'

Chelsea dragged her gaze back towards Dom, and managed a light laugh. 'Why not?' She took his proffered arm, and together they wove their way across the room.

'Oh, *Chelsea*!' Krysia greeted her with a perfunctory display of manners. 'It's been ages since I last saw you!'

'Two years,' Chelsea returned solemnly. 'How are you?'

The young girl lifted her shoulders and shimmied—there was no other word to describe the elegant graceful shiver that shook her slim frame.

'Fantastic!' Her lips formed a pretty pout. 'Raf tells me you're back together.'

'Yes.' There was no point in denying it, especially with Raf standing close by her side. Even as Chelsea uttered that single affirmative he caught hold of her hand and lifted it to his lips in a deliberately blatant gesture that brought twin flags of colour to her cheeks.

'Such enthusiasm!' drawled Raf with an edge of mockery, and she dredged up a stunning smile.

'This *is* a rather public place,' she managed lightly. 'I'm sure you can wait until we get home.'

His eyes gleamed with hidden laughter, and she stood transfixed as he lowered his head to hers and brushed his lips across her own in a warm, evocative gesture. 'Mm, perhaps we could leave early?'

Her mouth trembled for an instant, and there was a strange ache behind her eyes as she fought back the prickle of angry tears. 'And disappoint Alyse?'

'It would be unforgivable, I agree,' he said solemnly, although his eyes sharpened fractionally as they caught the sudden paleness of her features. 'Can I get you a drink?'

Chelsea nodded in acquiescence. 'Please.' It would steady her nerves and give her something to do with her hands. Besides, the evening had scarcely begun, and if she was to appear convincing she needed every vestige of courage she could summon—and then some!

Turning towards the younger girl, she queried

lightly 'What do you do, Krysia?'

'Oh—*modelling*,' Dom's daughter responded in bored tones, as if there could be no question of her doing anything else. 'That's why I'm here, *and* shopping while Daddy's tied up with business associates.' She tossed her head and the long mane of dark sable hair gleamed beneath the lights. 'Actually, I'll only be back in the States a week, then I fly off to Paris.'

'How exciting for you!' It was strange, but Chelsea really meant it. 'Paris is a wonderful city—I love it there. It possesses such a tremendous ambience, and the women are so *chic*!'

'I agree,' drawled Raf, and Chelsea felt a strange prickling sensation as all her fine body hairs tingled into awareness of his presence.

She looked at him and saw the warmth reflected in his features, the sheer sensuality evident, and for a moment she couldn't breathe as memories flooded her brain, taunting, vivid, and unmistakably painful.

Their honeymoon in France's capital city had been rapturous, everything she had ever dreamed and more, much more, for Raf had been a skilled and patient lover, and beneath his tutorage she had become an avid pupil.

'Thanks.' She took the glass from his outstretched hand and took a long swallow, grateful for its soothing effect.

'Perhaps we can get together before you leave?' Raf queried of the older man. 'I'll call you tomorrow.'

'Socially,' Krysia insisted huskily. 'With Daddy, it's always business.' She wrinkled her nose and cast Raf a conspiratorial glance. 'I'll make sure I'm free to join you.'

'Come, Krysia,' her father directed with amused resignation. 'We must circulate.'

'Another conquest, *darling*,' Chelsea murmured the instant they were out of earshot.

'I didn't covet it,' Raf declared drily, and she lifted her chin, meeting his dark gaze with equanimity.

To give him his due, he hadn't fostered Krysia's fascination, but then he hadn't needed to, she decided ruefully. Possessed of an elusive alchemy, he would always attract the opposite sex, and mixed with an aura of power and unlimited wealth his appeal was irresistible. If she was confident of his love, she might be amused. As it was, she had great difficulty in suppressing unenviable pangs of jealousy.

'Shall we mingle? Although I'm agreeable to playing the adoring wife, I find it infinitely more easy to do so in the company of others.' She glanced around the room, and gave a light, tinkling laugh. 'I guess we don't have to move an inch. We're about to be invaded by another of your feminine *friends*.' Her mouth widened into a warm smile that didn't quite reach her eyes. 'Perhaps I should go in search of a few of *my* friends—masculine, of course.' She was mad, she decided, for even thinking such a thing, let alone putting it into words.

'I'm tempted to shake you, do you know that?'

'My word!' Chelsea pretended to look horrified. 'Physical violence, Raf? If you'd consider such an act in public, whatever would you do when we're on our own?'

'Conduct a much more subtle punishment,' Raf

returned with glittering cynicism.

'Good heavens!' Chelsea admonished mildly. 'Can I accept that as a threat or a promise?'

'Continue treading such dangerous ground, and you'll surely find out.'

'Raf! I didn't believe it when they told me you were in Australia.'

'Georgina,' Chelsea greeted her, her smile firmly in place. 'How nice to see you again!'

'Yes, sweetheart, isn't it?' The tall, willowy, titian-haired actress offered a saccharin smile before centring her attention on Raf. 'How long has it been? Two months, three?' Her expression became distinctly wistful. 'You really should have phoned, darling. I sat around my New York hotel waiting ages for your call.'

Sweetheart, *darling*—suddenly it was all too much. Chelsea flashed them each a brilliant glance, then excused herself on the pretext of a necessary visit to the powder-room.

Once there, she took much longer than was necessary, tidying her hair, repairing her make-up, and when she re-entered the lounge she didn't resist being drawn into conversation with a group of men, among whom were three of Sam's closest friends.

Perhaps she had acquired a new maturity out of necessity, she mused absently, for during the past two years she had become accustomed to socialising without a man by her side. There had been occasions when Jonathan had partnered her to business functions, and away from the thrust and parry of the American scene she had regained much of her self-confidence.

'Chelsea! All on your own?'

She paused in the process of moving from one group to another, and turned slightly to meet Bryce's faintly curious expression 'The last time I looked, Raf was talking to Georgina.' A conspiratorial smile tugged the corner of her mouth. 'I thought I'd escape and leave him to cope alone.'

His kindly features creased into an answering grin. 'Ah, yes. Georgina can be—daunting, shall we say?'

'Definitely.'

'If you'll excuse me?' queried Bryce, catching his wife's flustered glance from a few feet distant. 'It appears I'm needed.'

Chelsea fingered the rim of her glass, then considered discarding it. The contents were lukewarm and watery with melted ice, and besides, she was no longer thirsty.

'Chelsea, darling—how are you?'

She turned to greet one of Sydney's prominent social hostesses, and found herself caught up in a skilfully manoeuvred *divertissement* elicited specifically to determine the reason for her sudden reconciliation with Raf. Something that was repeated several times as curiosity proved an overpowering drawcard for her attention.

It all seemed so superficial, and she felt as if her facial muscles were becoming stiff from continually maintaining an artificial façade. Her attention wandered, her eyes skimming the room as she unconsciously sought out a particular, dark well-groomed head, and her stomach executed a painful somersault as she glimpsed Raf deep in conversation with a tall, beautiful blonde. Almost as if he sensed her scrutiny, he glanced up, and a lump rose in her throat as a slow smile tugged the edge of his mouth. She watched in seeming fascination as he murmured something to his companion, then gradually began easing his way across the room.

A shaft of sheer sensation manifested itself deep inside her, slowly radiating until her whole body seemed alive with it. Even her hand shook as she reached for another drink from the tray of a passing waiter, yet by the time Raf reached her side she'd gathered together the shreds of her composure, sufficient to summon a brilliant smile as she turned to greet him.

'Raf, *darling*! Have you come to rescue me?'

'My dear Chelsea, you appear to be doing very well on your own,' he drawled, his features assembled into an expression of lazy warmth, although there was a dark, slumbrous quality lurking in the depths of his eyes which had little to do with passion.

Lifting a hand, Chelsea plucked an imaginary speck from the lapel of his suit jacket and pretended to examine it. 'Most of the people here formed part of my father's social circle,' she said steadily, then resentment flared. 'What would you have had me do, Raf? Stay with you and fight off the steady stream of women who are determined to lay claim to your attention?' Her eyes sparked with hidden fire. 'Sorry, but I'm not that charitable!'

'Krysia is Dom's *daughter*,' he retorted, as if that fact alone was sufficient explanation. 'Georgina——'

'Is one of Sam's ex-playmates,' Chelsea finished with a slight grimace. 'Who flits like a butterfly from one wealthy suitor to the next.'

His expression didn't alter, but his eyes hardened into dark obsidian chips. 'Are you suggesting I might have been involved with her?'

The silkiness in his voice should have been sufficient warning, but she was too consumed with icy rage to take any heed. '*Might*, Raf?' She gave a humourless laugh. 'Georgina seemed piqued that you didn't phone, remember?' she taunted, and felt a frisson of fear slither the length of her spine at his long, hard glance.

'Be sure of your facts before you fling any accusations, Chelsea.'

Her chin tilted fractionally. 'What *are* the facts, Raf? I'm all ears.'

For a few fateful seconds they seemed locked in silent battle, and she couldn't have looked away if her life depended upon it.

'Georgina happened to be in the same restaurant in downtown Manhattan while I was dining with friends,' he told her brusquely. 'She joined us for a while, and when we left she slipped me her telephone number.' His gaze raked hers, harsh and terrifyingly implacable. 'I chose to ignore the invitation.'

Chelsea unconsciously released her breath, then snapped with more than a trace of cynicism, 'How incredibly noble of you!'

'Don't be sarcastic!'

The strain of projecting a façade was becoming intolerable and, she said so, adding wretchedly, 'I'd like to go home!'

'Alyse is about to serve supper,' Raf observed. 'And we have yet to dance together.'

Supper? *Dance*? She couldn't face eating a single thing, and as for dancing—she doubted she could bear being held in his arms without betraying something of her inner turmoil.

The food was exquisitely presented, and she stood at Raf's side as he made a careful selection from various platters, and when he offered her a morsel she accepted it into her mouth without thought, aware of the implied intimacy and hating him for it.

She talked, keeping up a conversational patter that was totally inconsequential, and afterwards she had no clear recollection of a word she had uttered. It was almost as if she was a silent spectator, aware of her words and actions, yet remote in a way that made her wonder if she hadn't imbibed one too many glasses of champagne!

'If I have to smile once more, I think my face will crack,' she murmured as Raf's arms enfolded her slim form close against him.

'Rest your head against my shoulder and we'll pretend to be totally absorbed in one another.'

Chelsea heard the faint cynicism in his voice and felt defeated. It would be so easy to melt in his arms, no need for any pretence. Her whole body seemed to possess a will of its own, as, unbidden, her breathing quickened fractionally, and a shivery sensation feathered its way down the length of her spine. Primeval sensuality at its most dangerous, she decided pensively. An explosive mesh of electric sexual energy and fiery passion that was based on physical lust.

'No adamant refusal?'

She glanced up and met his dark, enigmatic gaze

with subdued solemnity. 'I think I'm through playing games for tonight.'

'Poor Chelsea,' he derided gently. 'Has it been so bad?'

'Yes,' she admitted simply. 'I feel as if I'm shattering into a million fragments.'

His head lowered fractionally as he brushed his lips against her temple. 'Never mind, *querida*. Tomorrow we'll take the boat out, and you can hate me as much as you like without a soul within sight or sound to overhear us.'

Chelsea experienced an intrinsic pull that had everything to do with the senses, and she lowered her lashes so that Raf couldn't glimpse the strength of her emotions. Held like this in his arms, she could almost believe the past two years didn't exist, that with no effort at all they could regain what they had lost. Yet there was no ignoring her inner voice as it demanded caution, for what was the use of lowering her guard and losing her heart all over again when within a matter of weeks, a few months at the most, he'd be gone? She had no illusions that the length of his stay was governed by the time it took to convince the majority of Houghton-Hamilton stockholders.

It was well after midnight when they made their farewells, and in the car Chelsea sat in silence, too enervated to bother uttering so much as a word as the Jaguar purred the quiet streets beneath Raf's competent hands.

As soon as he brought the car to a halt in the garage, she quickly released the door-clasp and slid from her seat, choosing to walk ahead as he attended to security measures. The fine hairs at the back of her neck prickled with apprehension as she moved indoors, and she made for the stairs without pausing, in a bid to reach the safety of her bedroom. Once there she closed the door and leant against it, her breathing as rapid as if she'd just run a smile.

A hollow laugh emerged from her throat. Safe, *here*, with no locks to bar Raf's entry? Who was she kidding, for heaven's sake?

All evening she had been playing a game, but the ultimate irony was that beneath the façade lay the bitter truth of love.

The knowledge made her movements jerky and uncoordinated as she slowly removed her clothes, and in the adjoining bathroom she stood in front of the mirror abstractedly examining her features, seeing the wide, haunted expression in her eyes, the pale features beneath what was left of her make-up. She looked like a wraith, she decided as she reached for her toothbrush and conducted a rigorous cleaning before sluicing her face with cold water.

Then she slipped into her nightgown and went back to her bedroom, determined to sleep despite the host of memories that invaded her brain. In bed she lay still, her ears unconsciously alert for the slightest sound that would indicate Raf had come upstairs.

After what seemed an interminable length of time she simply closed her eyes, willing an escape into blissful somnolence. Perhaps her guardian angel smiled in assent, for she came sharply awake from the edge of a vivid dream to discover it was daylight.

CHAPTER SIX

A GLANCE at the bedside clock revealed that it was shortly after seven o'clock, and for a moment Chelsea lay still, luxuriating in the fact that it was Sunday and she didn't have to rise early. Then she remembered Raf's intention to take *Mystique* out on to the harbour, and a silent groan emerged from her lips. Oh, why hadn't she refused last night to accompany him, instead of indicating a tacit acceptance by virtue of saying *nothing*? Because, an impertinent imp inside her head taunted, you were enmeshed in an emotional spell at the time, and afterwards you didn't even *think*!

Well, the only thing to do was tell him she wasn't going, and with that thought in mind she slid out of bed, showered, then she quickly dressed in denim shorts and added a shocking-pink top before hurrying downstairs.

All the doors leading out on to the terraced patio were open, and Chelsea could see Raf seated beneath a shaded umbrella, coffee-cup in hand, with the Sunday papers spread out on the table.

He glanced up as she moved through the doorway, and she felt a strange prickling sensation as his eyes skimmed slowly up the tanned length of her legs to rest with barely disguised mockery on her expressive features.

'Good morning. I was beginning to think I'd have to invade your bedroom and wake you.'

Imagining just how he'd effect that awakening, and the pleasure he'd derive from her sleepy vulnerability, put a fine edge on her temper.

'Orange juice?' He closed the newspaper and put it down on a nearby chair. 'Do sit down, Chelsea,' he said easily as he poured freshly squeezed juice into a glass. 'Hannah has provided your usual cereal and milk, and there's at least two more cups of coffee in the pot.'

Perhaps if she had the orange juice first, she could then gain strength from the aromatic coffee before launching into a defensive as to why she wasn't going out on the boat with him. Yet, when the moment came, she sounded stilted and incredibly formal.

'I've decided not to go with you today.' There, she'd said it! What was more, she held his piercing scrutiny with wide-eyed determination.

This morning he looked vaguely piratical, attired in white shorts, a casual pin-striped black and white shirt, with dark glasses shading his eyes against the sun.

'*Mystique* is fuelled and ready,' Raf told her silkily. 'A day of relaxation will do you good.'

'I relaxed yesterday at the beach,' she responded tightly. 'Besides, I won't be dictated to.'

'Quit while you're ahead, Chelsea. Perversity for the sheer hell of it is pointless.'

Fury welled up inside her and she became intensely angry, hurling with supressed vehemence, 'You can't walk calmly back into my life and attempt to take over! Besides, I refuse to be manipulated like an inanimate puppet!'

'Have you finished?'

'No—*yes*, damn you. And I'm not going!'

'You are. Of your own free will, or hoisted over my shoulder. The choice is yours.'

'Whatever will Hannah think?'

His smile was entirely without humour. 'Imagine we've had a slight tiff, and I'm being very masterful in remedying it.'

'Tyrannical is more apt!'

Raf sat there totally at ease and apparently unaffected by her acerbity. 'Finish your breakfast. We're leaving in ten minutes.'

Chelsea replaced her cup and stood to her feet. 'I'm leaving, but not with you.' She'd go to the beach again, or visit friends—anything. As long as she could do it without his unsufferable presence. All she needed was a skirt and her shoulder-bag, both of which were upstairs in her room, and without a further word she made her way indoors to retrieve them.

She'd darn well call his bluff, she decided as she ran lightly downstairs a few minutes later, and in the garage she walked over to the Porsche and slid in behind the wheel—only to discover her keys were not in the ignition.

'Looking for something?'

Chelsea glanced up and met Raf's cynical expression, and knew without doubt that he had removed them.

'You *bastard*! Give me my keys!'

'Will agreed that today would provide an excellent

opportunity for him to wash your car.'

Almost shaking with anger, Chelsea slipped out and closed the door, then without thought her hand swung in an upward arc to connect with a resounding crack against the side of his face.

Shock kept her immobile for several heartstopping seconds, and she gave a silent cry of pain as his hands slid up to fasten over her shoulders in a bruising grip.

'No—*don't!*'

But it was too late for any appeal, and she glimpsed the icy resolve in Raf's long, hard glance, then his head lowered with deadly intent, and his mouth subjugated hers in an invasion that was pitilessly cruel—punishing, libidinous, and almost savagely merciless.

Her mouth ached, its delicate inner tissue grazed and tender, her tongue swollen from his ravaging possession, and even the ribs hurt beneath the iron-like grasp of his arm as he locked her slim frame against his own.

She could hardly breathe, let alone move, and after the first few annihilating seconds she gave up attempting to struggle against him. Not once, *ever*, had he kissed her quite like this, and just as she thought it would never stop he relinquished her mouth and put her at arm's length, where she stood pale and swaying and quite unable to utter so much as a word.

A husky, indiscernible expletive left his lips, and his eyes darkened until they resembled polished onyx as she silently gazed at him, then he reached for her hand and led her to the Jaguar, opened the door and pushed her gently into the passenger seat before crossing round to slip in behind the wheel.

Chelsea sat in silence as he fired the engine and sent the large car purring down the driveway, and she didn't so much as demur when he brought the Jaguar to a halt in the parking area adjacent the inner harbour marina where *Mystique* lay at its moorings.

Rather than have the luxurious vessel lie idle after Sam's death, Chelsea had leased her out to a charter firm, and now she pondered *Mystique's* availability at such short notice. Without doubt Raf's considerable influence was responsible, she decided ruminatively as she walked at his side and then preceded him on board.

Within minutes the powerful engines throbbed into life, and she tensed slightly as he curtly requested her to cast off. The temptation to tell him to do it himself was stifled as she quickly tended to the ropes, then she moved to the stern to view their departure, watching absently as the marina grew smaller and smaller, until it faded out of sight.

Raf had forced her on board, but that didn't mean she had to go up front and be with him while he steered *Mystique* out into the harbour. There had to be some magazines, a few books, in the cabin lounge, and if not—well, she'd simply stretch out on deck and improve her tan. The only time they'd have to talk would be when he dropped anchor for lunch, and until then she would enjoy her own solitude.

The cabin lounge revealed a few glossy magazines, some featuring fashion design, others accenting interior decorating. Interest was responsible for her tour of inspection, noting the neatly assembled bunks in the three cabins, the impeccably maintained appointments, and she felt an incredible sense of sadness, for Sam had revelled in his role as host, and *Mystique* had been the venue for many a party that she could remember, and probably several that she had never had the opportunity to participate in during her scholastic career.

She wandered into the galley, idly opening cupboards, noting their contents and the well-stocked bar-fridge. That today's sojourn had been well planned was evident, and she experienced a strange sense of trepidation. Raf was a complex man, highly respected among his associates and deliberately sought by the fairer sex. Yet he managed to project an aloofness mingled with impeccable courtesy, almost a personal distancing that most women found intensely intriguing, providing a desire to delve beneath the surface and discover for themselves what manner of man lay behind the mask.

Chelsea wondered if even *she* knew. Certainly he was many things—kind, considerate, passionate. He could also be hard and implacable, as he had been this morning, unleashing a controlled violence that even now had the capacity to make her feel shivery with inexplicable fear. Yet beneath that frightening onslaught she had sensed an angry impatience, almost as if he sought to shock her into some kind of self-discovery.

Oh, *hell*! What on earth was the matter with her, for heaven's sake? Raf needed her visible compliance, nothing more, and he was prepared to go to any lengths to get it.

Crossing back into the cabin lounge, she determinedly collected a few magazines, some sunscreen cream, and went back up on deck, where she settled herself comfortably in a canvas chair to read undisturbed.

Occasionally her attention wandered out over the bay, noting several pleasure craft of varying size and design taking advantage of the warm balmy weather and excellent sailing conditions.

It really was tremendously relaxing, the sun, the soft almost mesmeric swell of the sea. If she closed her eyes she was almost sure she'd drift into a light doze. Perhaps that was the answer, to shut out, even temporarily, the problems Raf's presence in her life represented.

There were images, shadowy and indistinguishable, fighting for supremacy inside her brain. Every now and again the shadows cleared and she caught glimpses of Raf, herself, in happier times. Just snatches of shared laughter, *love*. Then there were the darker images, pain, and memories she had no wish to remember.

Suddenly she felt cool, as if a shadow had blocked out the sun, and her eyes slowly flickered open in silent protest, then dilated as they focused on the source of her lack of warmth. Standing close in front of her was Raf, his broad frame vaguely threatening, and she blinked, her long-fringed lashes lowering in a protective gesture.

For what seemed an age he didn't utter so much as a word, then he thrust his hands into the pockets of his shorts. 'I've put down anchor. We can go ashore and have lunch on the beach, or eat here. Which would you prefer?'

Lunch? It couldn't be midday already, surely? But it was, she saw with incredulity as she cast a quick glance at her watch. She'd never felt less like eating in her life, and as to where—she didn't particularly want to be prey to the dozens of pairs of eyes of those picnicking on the beach, nor did she want to be alone with him on board. Yet clearly it had to be one or the other.

'Here.' Chelsea deliberately refrained from looking at him directly, aiming instead for a point in the vicinity of his left shoulder, and she flinched as he reached out and brushed his fingers against her arms.

'You've caught the sun.'

She managed a seemingly careless shrug as she inspected the pinkened flush beneath her tan. 'I'll apply some more cream.' He didn't move, and she felt her breathing quicken slightly at his dark, unfathomable expression. For a moment she could almost believe she glimpsed regret, then the moment was gone as he turned and made his way down into the cabin lounge.

Chelsea followed suit, going to the galley to extract a selection of cold meats, chicken, and a variety of fresh salad from the refrigerator while Raf set the table with plates and cutlery. There were crunchy bread rolls, and chilled wine to accompany the meal, although she didn't feel in the slightest bit hungry and merely forked a few mouthfuls of chicken, played with the lettuce, and crumbled up part of a bread roll.

'You are aware we're dining with Dom tonight?'

The tenuous hold she had on her fragile emotions slipped a fraction, for in truth Dom's dinner invitation had gone right out of her mind. 'I'd forgotten.'

She attempted civility and just attained it by the skin of her teeth. 'I imagine Krysia will be there?'

One eyebrow rose in a gesture of wry cynicism. 'You have any objection if she is?'

Yes, damn you! Chelsea seethed silently. It was bad enough maintaining a pretence, without having to put up with the young girl's fawning infatuation! 'Not to her actual presence, no,' she said with complete honesty, and managed to hold Raf's gaze as it raked her features.

'Dom flies back to the States early tomorrow. Unfortunately, he won't be able to come to our party.'

'But Krysia will, of course.' The words fell glibly from her lips, and quite frankly she didn't care if she sounded bitchy.

'Are you suggesting I should tell her she isn't welcome?'

'Heaven forbid! Why not invite every smitten female you can think of, and provide her with plenty of competition?' As soon as the words fell from her lips she regretted them, but it was too late to retract, and she saw his eyes narrow. Steady, she cautioned. If she wasn't careful, she'd only heap more retribution on her hapless head. His chastisement only brief hours before had been ruthlessly explicit, and she had no inclination to suffer a similar punishment.

'Anyone would think I deliberately seek the company of women, when the reverse is true,' Raf drawled cynically, and his dark eyes sharpened and became infinitely compelling. 'You're extremely beautiful, and yet if I were to accuse you of consciously attracting the attention of men, you'd offer an angry denial.'

Chelsea merely lifted her glass and sipped the icy fruit juice, enjoying its sharp tang.

'No comment?'

There was a hard ruthlessness beneath the surface and despite the warmth within the cabin, a chill sensation shivered its way over her skin.

'What do you want me to say, Raf?' Her nerves felt on edge, and as taut as a tightly stretched piece of wire. 'There are some men with whom I feel perfectly at ease. Others who make me feel vaguely uncomfortable.' She forced herself to meet his studied gaze. 'I don't create sexual tension and utilise it as a weapon. It isn't my style.'

'Are you suggesting that it's mine?'

Chelsea drained the glass and replaced it on the table. 'I think,' she said heavily, 'that you make your own rules and suit them to any given occasion.' Her eyes never left his as he leaned well back in his chair.

'Accusations, Chelsea?'

'If you like.' She felt reckless, almost uncaring.

Raf studied her for several heartstopping seconds, then drawled silkily, 'Elucidate.'

'Stop being my inquisitor!' she threw a trifle wildly. 'I don't want to be here with you, and I most certainly don't want to join Dom and Krysia for dinner tonight. You can damn well go alone!' In one angry movement she rose to her feet and was about to escape back up on deck when her wrist was captured in a steely grip that held her immobile and volubly seething. 'Let me go!'

'You'd try the patience of a saint, do you know that? One minute Little Miss Cool, the next a veritable volcano!' Raf stood to his feet and moved round the table. 'I'm almost inclined to ask which is the real Chelsea Hamilton.'

'Oh—*both*,' she flung caustically. 'It's the effect you create.' Fool, she thought hollowly. Don't you know you can never win? Anger had never achieved anything in the past, and it wasn't likely to now. She jerked her wrist, trying to break free of his grasp, and gave an angry cry of pain. 'Damn you, Raf! You're hurting me!'

'Stop it,' he cautioned hardily. 'If you don't, I'll treat you like the child you are.'

'Lay one hand on me, and I'll have you up for assault!' Chelsea snapped vengefully, and saw his eyes darken with anger.

'Wife-beating?' A short, humourless laugh escaped his throat. 'Oh no, nothing so painfully physically. I'm sure I can summon something much more—imaginatively subtle than hauling you across my knee,' he drawled, pulling her so close that she could smell the faint musky aroma of his aftershave, feel the sheer strength in his muscular, hard frame.

Without any effort at all he caught both her hands together behind her back, then he lowered his head to the hollow at the curve of her neck, brushing the sensitised flesh with his open mouth before trailing up to caress the edge of her jaw. Her cotton top proved no barrier to his hand, and she cried out as he cupped her breast, then deviously unhooked the front fastening of her bra, freeing the creamy fullness and allowing him licence to the burgeoning rosy peaks which hardened damnably at his lightest touch.

Already her traitorous body was awakening, fuelled by a flame that had never really died, and she moaned softly, hating, loving him, wanting, *aching* for so much more.

Yet, when his mouth slowly travelled down towards one soft mound, she jerked back, afraid, and struggled fruitlessly as he teased the tender roseate nub with his tongue before taking it into his mouth to render an exquisite havoc that made her want to cry out in futile frustration.

Then, just as she thought she was going crazy with need, he let his lips trail a path to her throat, and she arched her head back, revelling in the series of open-mouthed kisses he bestowed until he reached the curve of her mouth.

Without thought she parted her lips in hungry welcome, flinching slightly as his tongue caught the grazed inner tissue where he'd callously kissed her earlier that morning. His touch was incredibly gentle, seducing with such delicate mastery her whole body seemed to pulse with liquid fire, and she became mindless, lost in a world of sensuality so intense she felt as if she was drawn into a swirling vortex where emotion ruled and reality belonged elsewhere.

Then suddenly she was free, and she looked at him in silent query, her eyes wide sleepy pools of green fire.

'The radio telephone,' said Raf suddenly, and she registered the staccato, repetitive burring sound with a sense of disbelief. 'I'll have to answer it. Will has instructions to relay anything of immediate importance.'

Chelsea nodded, too caught up in a mesmeric thrall

to trust herself to speak. Her lips shook slightly, and she was powerless to move as he leant down and gave her a brief hard kiss, then turned and strode quickly towards the control-room.

She hugged her arms together as reaction began to take its toll, and realisation of what might have happened between them had it not been for the telephone's timely intervention. To be brought to such a fever pitch of sexual pleasure, then denied its ultimate conclusion, left her feeling shattered and incomplete, and the aching tremors of her body were a damnable reminder of the power he retained. With very little effort he could reduce her to a willing supplicant, eager, wanton, and all too ready to please and be pleasured. *Why not?* a devilish imp prompted. What was so wrong in wanting to slake a physical need?

Except where did it leave her afterwards? Feeling slightly sickened, she stirred herself sufficiently to clear away the remains of their lunch and wash the dishes.

She had just finished the chore when she heard Raf come back into the cabin, and she felt incredibly vulnerable as her fine body hairs prickled into awareness of his presence. Her hands shook as she wiped down the stainless-steel sink, and there was nothing she could do to stop the slight tremor that raked her slender frame when Raf slid his arms round her waist from behind.

'Such domestic dedication!' he murmured with a husky laugh as he buried his lips against the sensitve edge of her neck. One hand splayed down over the flatness of her stomach, while the other shifted beneath her top and captured her breast. 'Hmm, you smell beautiful,' he breathed softly as he gently nuzzled the pulsing cord, then began a slow assault on her nape before trailing to the delicate hollows beneath her collarbone, 'and taste delicious.'

It was an insidious conflagration of the senses and infinitely treacherous, arousing a primitive desire over which Chelsea was fast losing control.

As he turned her round to face him, her hands fluttered up towards his shoulders, then slipped down the muscular length of his arms. 'Raf——'

Her protest was stifled as his mouth closed over hers, warm, seductive and incredibly gentle. Warning bells sounded in the deep recesses of her mind, and she gave a silent groan of despair, knowing that if she didn't heed them *now* she'd be hopelessly lost.

With a sense of desolation she tore her mouth away and let her head sink against the curve of his shoulder as she drew in deep gulps of air and made some attempt to control the deep tremors that swept through her body.

How long she stayed there she had little recollection. It could have been minutes, or mere seconds, and she was powerless to resist the faint pressure as Raf caught her chin and tilted it, forcing her to meet his gaze.

Her eyes widened, then became cloudy with pain, and she swallowed convulsively as his hands framed her face. With infinite gentleness he caressed the softly parted curve of her mouth, letting his fingers trace an evocative pattern over the slightly swollen contours, and she felt a dull ache begin at the back of her eyes as they misted with unshed tears.

Oh, dear lord, what was the matter with her? She swung like a pendulum between rebellion and raw desire, wanting, *needing* him with such intensity it was slowly driving her insane.

'What is it to be, Chelsea? A comfortable bed in one of the cabins, or do we go back up on deck and pretend we don't share a mutal need?'

How could she say—*I can't? Because if I do, I'll never be able to survive when you leave.*

Somehow she manged to dredge up a shaky smile 'Whatever happened to male persuasion?'

'Are you suggesting I should sweep you into my arms, stride into the nearest room, then kick the door shut and have my wicked way with you?' he countered. 'Is that what you want?'

She felt infinitely fragile, ready to break in two if he should exert the slightest pressure. Drawing a deep breath, she held it briefly, then slowly released it. 'No,' she denied through a throat constricted with pain.

Raf's eyes darkened measurably, then he leant forward and brushed her mouth with his own. 'Then let's go back up on deck and try our hand at catching some fish. I had Will include the rods and all the relevant gear.'

It was a relief to move back into the sunshine, and Chelsea busied herself fixing hooks and sinkers to the nylon lines, while Raf attended to the bait.

For the ensuing two hours they enjoyed a camaraderie that stripped away several of the protective layers she had painstakingly assembled over the past two years in defence against him, and she wondered, not for the first time, if this seemingly relaxed man and the forceful executive who wielded power with such effortless ease in the hi-tech business world were one and the same.

'What's your verdict?'

Cheslea looked momentarily startled at his drawling query, then she let her head tilt slightly to one side and ventured musingly, 'On the dynamic corporate director?'

'How about—Raf Hamilton, the man?'

Why did she feel as if she'd suddenly skated on to perilously thin ice? 'Is it possible to separate the two?'

'Yet you enjoy a position of executive power,' Raf reminded her, subjecting her to a penetrating scrutiny. 'Do you allow it to spill over into your private life?'

What private life? She suppressed a tiny grimace. Unless you counted the meaningless round of parties, the social circuit which included attending the theatre, the opera. Sam's house had become her own, a sanctuary where she could relax and be herself. But there were occasions when she became restless with its emptiness, nights when she was filled with desperate longing for a man to share it all with, even indulging wistful thoughts of children eventually. Several men were more than willing, and had professed an eager desire to do so, dismissing her gold, diamond-encrusted wedding band as a mere formality that could be easily dispensed with. Except that Chelsea hadn't been able to overlook it, just as she could never dismiss the man who had placed it there.

'Perhaps I'm not sufficiently entrenched within the

corporate structure to have paid my dues,' she responded lightly.

'And if you were?'

'I'd ensure I kept them separate as much as possible,' Chelsea said carefully. 'Quality time is more important than quantity.'

'Ah, an astute female!'

'The days when a woman was confined to the kitchen through lack of choice, raising a family and catering to her man's slightest whim, no longer exist.'

Raf spared her a twisted smile. 'That's a weighty statement, and not entirely true. There are a number of women who, through lack of financial support, do not have that choice.'

'You're including *all* women,' she corrected. 'I intended a broad generalisation aimed at those who can afford to attain the educational qualifications that provide them with an entrée into their chosen field. You must admit there are a great number of women who handle their work competently.'

'Are you trying to say that given a choice between corporate success and a family life, you'd choose success?'

'Not necessarily,' she said slowly. 'I'd like both, allowing a shift in priorities as the situation demanded, an aligning which could be achieved with domestic help and flexible office hours. In any case, the way technology is advancing, it will soon be possible for a number of women to work from within their home environment.'

'And where does that leave the male of the species?'

'Enriched, I would say. With a partner whose self-esteem is satisfied, therefore self-confidence is at a comparable level. Knowledge, equality regarding understanding of each other's work and the ability for discussion.' Chelsea paused, then ticked off a fourth finger. 'Mutual respect.'

'So you view women in the sole role of homemaker as a diminishing force?'

'Not at all. There are a number of women who take tremendous pride in their home and family, and see it as their fulfilment in life.'

'But not you?' Raf parried with slight mockery, and she looked at him carefully, attempting to assess his precise meaning.

'I don't think it's applicable,' she answered slowly.

'No? You hold a directorship in a highly successful company, and you're married. I would have said it's extremely pertinent.'

Too late she saw that he had very effectively set a trap into which she had fallen head-first. 'But it *isn't* pertinent,' she denied. 'Because we're not really married.'

'Indeed? I have a legal certificate in my possession to prove that we are.'

'Legally the marriage is still valid, but we lead separate lives.'

'We occupy the same house.'

'Only to perpetrate an illusion,' she responded quickly, and saw the edge of his mouth curve with amusement.

'I'm quite willing to make the change to reality.'

'Oh, I'm sure you are! It would be very convenient if I were to accommodate you sexually, wouldn't it?' Her eyes became brilliant with emerald fire. 'Damn you to hell, Raf! I lived with you as your wife for almost two years, and it was like riding a tiger. I fell off so many times, it nearly killed me.' She backed away from him, almost like an animal being manoeuvred into a corner. 'If you want sexual satisfaction, go and find it with someone else!'

'Ah, but you see I don't want anyone else.'

It took several seconds for his words to sink in, and she looked at him, her eyes widening until they became huge green pools of incredulity. She felt as if time lay suspended as the silence between them assumed an electrifying quality, and she couldn't have moved if her life depended upon it.

'I do believe we've caught something!' Raf declared as one of the rods began to bend, and Chelsea looked at him in stunned disbelief, unable to assimilate the swift change from sublimity to something as mundane as the prospect of a fishing catch.

The other rod suffered a similar fate, and within a short time there were no fewer than ten good-sized fish lying in an ice-packed polystyrene container.

'Shall we head for home? It's almost three, and by the time we get back we shall have an hour to shower and change and drive into the city to meet Dom.'

The thought of spending an evening with one of Raf's valued associates was daunting, especially when Krysia was sure to be an inclusion. Having to bear witness to the young girl's overt flirting was more than Chelsea could endure, and as *Mystique* sliced through the relatively smooth waters of Broken Bay she devised the invention of a headache as an excuse to escape the dinner invitation.

However, when they reached Castlecrag it became

clearly evident there was no need for invention. A headache had obligingly manifested itself, clouding her eyes with pain and imbuing her features with a pallor that was totally uncontrived. Perhaps it was auto-suggestion, Chelsea decided, or one of those tension headaches. Dear heaven, she'd surely been under enough emotional pressure since Raf's sudden reappearance in her life!

Rather wearily she made her way indoors, leaving Raf to help Will unload the supplies they'd taken on board and their fishing catch.

Upstairs in her room she crossed to the bedroom and turned on the shower, then she opened the medicine cabinet, extracted two Paracetamol tablets and swallowed them with water. Removing her clothes, she got into the smoky-tinted glass cubicle to stand beneath the steady pulsing jet as she lathered her skin and her hair, before taking an inordinate length of time to rinse off.

Towelled dry, she completed her toilette, donned a silk robe over her nightgown, then she crossed to the house-phone in order to alert Hannah that she would be down later to poach herself an egg on toast—all the dinner she felt able to stomach.

Now all she had to do was inform Raf. Which might not be as easy as she envisaged, and decided seconds later as she paused tentatively outside his bedroom. The door was open, and at that moment he turned, shooting her a slightly mocking, interrogative glance.

'Problems?'

Her eyes took in the dark, hip-hugging trousers, the white shirt he was in the process of buttoning, and she had trouble meeting his gaze.

'I've developed a headache, it started on the way home. I've already taken tablets, but they haven't had much effect.' She was aware she was babbling, but she couldn't stop herself: 'I really don't feel well enough to go out.'

She saw his eyes narrow fractionally, and had to force herself not to step backwards as he crossed the room and stood far too close for her comfort.

'Fact or fiction, Chelsea?'

At that moment a shaft of pain radiated from behind her right eye, and she winced at its ferocity. 'Fact, damn you,' she acknowledged shakily.

'I'll phone Dom and cancel.'

'Don't be silly—I'll be perfectly fine. Besides,' she added, finding it difficult to regulate her breathing, 'Dom will be disappointed.' She didn't say *and Krysia*, but the thought was there, and she saw the darkness intensify in the depth of his eyes. 'I've already told Hannah.'

Raf moved back towards the bed, fastened the last of his shirt buttons, then caught up a tie and deftly knotted it. 'I'll leave the name and number of the restaurant in case you need to call.'

Chelsea stifled a faint grimace. 'I'm only suffering from a headache, not pneumonia!'

He crossed into the en-suite bathroom and she watched as he groomed his hair. It was an intensely masculine action, but it fascinated her, and the sharp aroma of freshly applied aftershave teased her nostrils. Then he re-entered the room, collected his jacket and slid his arms into it before pocketing his wallet.

'Why don't you get into bed, and I'll have Hannah send up a tray?' He walked towards her, and for one heartstopping, contrary moment she wished she was going with him.

'No, I'll eat something downstairs.' She held her breath as he subjected her to a raking appraisal, then he smiled and brushed his lips against her temple.

'I'll see you at breakfast. Dont bother going into the office in the morning if you don't feel up to it.'

He turned, moving with an easy, lithe grace from the room, and minutes later Chelsea heard the muted purr of the Jaguar's engine as he sent the powerful car down towards the gates.

With a heavy sigh she walked through to her own room and switched on the portable television. There was a pile of books reposing on the pedestal beside her bed, and if television or reading palled she could certainly do with an early night.

An hour later, propped up against the pillows and sipping hot sweet tea, she used the remote control unit to switch off a particularly gruesome news item, and selected a book. That didn't hold her interest for very long either, and she slid out of bed and padded into the bathroom for another dose of Paracetamol. Then she determinedly plumped her pillows, slipped in between the sheets and plunged out the beside light.

She must have slept, for she came sharply awake from a terrifyingly vivid dream and simply lay there, wide-eyed and firmly enmeshed in a totally alien sequence which had no possible bearing on her past or the present.

Her eyes sought the luminous hands on the clock resting on the pedestal next to her bed. Midnight. Was Raf home yet? Damn. She wouldn't check and see. Besides, she didn't care whether he was in or not.

Perhaps if she read for a while it would take her mind off the after-effects of her bad dream. Suiting thought to action, she reached out and switched on the light, then picked up her book and determinedly read until her eyes began to blur. A drink, and another two tablets. Her headache was reducing to a mere niggle, but the medication would help her get back to sleep.

On her way back from the bathroom she stopped still with shock at the sight of Raf standing calmly in the middle of the room.

'What are you doing here?' she demanded incredulously, and glimpsed his faintly narrowed gaze as it roved with deliberate appraisal over her slim curves. The satin-finished silk wrap clung lovingly to her breasts, and her fingers automatically adjusted the stitched edges, then slid down to tighten the belt. She could feel the anger welling up inside her until it threatened to erupt. How dared he calmly walk into her bedroom as if he had the right to do so?

'Merely checking that you hadn't fallen asleep with the light on,' he drawled indolently, although there was nothing remotely lazy in his expression.

How could she go to sleep when he was still out at—*two* in the morning? So much for *dinner* with an important associate!

'I was reading.' She turned slightly and pointed to a book lying open on the bed.

'Standing up?'

His mocking amusement positively incensed her, and it was a miracle that she could speak. 'What is this? An interrogation?' Her eyes warred openly with his, and she took a deep, calming breath. 'I got out of bed to get a glass of water from the bathroom.'

He was silent for so long, she began to wonder if he intended uttering another word.

'Dom asked me to convey his sympathy,' Raf told her, 'and express his regret at not being able to see you again before he returns to the States.' His gaze became faintly brooding. 'I should have cancelled and stayed with you.

'And spoiled your fun?

'Would you care to qualify that?' His voice resembled velvet-encased steel, and Chelsea suppressed a shiver of apprehension.

'I'm sure you managed admirably in my absence.'

With the utmost care he turned to close the door, and at the dull clunking sound her stomach performed a series of painful somersaults.

'Krysia?' His smile was the antithesis of anything resembling amusement. 'Dom's daughter is a delightful child.'

'Oh, really, Raf,' she chided mockingly, 'there's nothing remotely childish about the way she regards *you*!'

'And that bothers you?'

'Not at all.' Liar, she chastised herself mentally. You've been so consumed with jealousy, you haven't been able to think of anything else all evening! Imagining Krysia's kittenish claws and the young girl's seductive ploy had prohibited any pretence of enjoyment.

'How is your headache?'

His mocking sarcasm was her undoing, and without thought she picked up a pillow from the bed and threw it at him, following it with another in quick succession, incensed to the point of blind rage.

'If you want to play, Chelsea,' he drawled, I'm quite willing to oblige.' With slow, unhurried movements he thrust the pillows down on to the bed and moved towards her, his hard, intent stare playing havoc with her composure.

A silent scream rose and died before it found voice at the unspoken threat in those chilling depths.

'No.' The sound came out as a husky whisper, and her eyes widened into large, stormy pools as he casually shrugged off his jacket and tossed it over a nearby chair. 'What do you think you're doing?' Her throat constricted with fear as he caught hold of her shoulders. She pushed against him and lost her balance as he fell back on to the bed, pulling her with him, and she began to struggle in earnest as his arms closed around her slim form, moving with disturbing ease to hold her fast against him.

'Let me go!' It was a desperate plea that went unheeded as she felt his hand slide up to cup the back of her head, forcing it down until her mouth was within touching distance of his own. 'Raf, don't—*please!*' The words were wrung from her in a tortured whisper as he rolled over, pinning her beneath him.

'Don't—*what?*' he murmured huskily. With a slow, featherlight touch he began to caress the hollows at the base of her throat, trailing his lips down the edge of her wrap. 'Do this?' Without any effort at all he slid the edges apart and moved his mouth with tantalising deliberation towards one rocky-peaked breast, beginning a teasing, exploratory circle before taking it into his mouth with the consummate ease she recognised. And her body began, damnably, of its own volition, to respond.

A slow ache started in the region of her stomach, steadily spreading to her loins as she threshed restlessly against the throbbing passion that pulsed like quicksilver through her veins.

Just when she thought she could bear no more, Raf shifted his attention to its twin, wreaking devastation of a kind she found impossible to ignore.

Not content, his mouth travelled up to cover her own, gently, and with such a wealth of seduction that he was able to evoke the very response she had sworn not to give.

A tortured groan escaped Chelsea's lips as he sought the heart of her femininity, playing the delicate sensory core with the mastery of a virtuoso, until she became a tormented, willing supplicant begging the release only his possession could assauge.

'Patience, my sweet,' Raf bade quietly as he moved to stand close to the bed's edge. 'While you are delightfully unclothed, I am still wearing most of mine.' He began divesting himself of them with unhurried deftness, his eyes never leaving hers for an instant.

In mesmerised fascination she admired the superb musculature of his body, the honed sinews that rippled strength with every move he made until, naked, he moved towards her, the heat of his arousal a potent, virile force.

Perhaps it was his animalistic sense of power that triggered a return to sanity at a moment when her flesh cried out in rejection to the message of panic issuing from her brain.

What was she *doing*, for heaven's sake? Lying supine and filled with a treacherous weakness, just waiting for him to effect the ultimate devastation, like an inanimate doll, lulled into a sense of false security by his sensual expertise.

And afterwards? What happened then? Would she simply slip into sharing his bed, accepting his love-making? A sob of self-derision rose damnably to the surface. *Lovemaking* meant making love, not merely a satiating of the senses that had lust as its seed. She'd trodden that particular path before, except that then she'd been too naïve to recognise love from lust, and had believed the two were irrevocably interwined . . .

'*No!*' The single negation emerged as an anguished cry, and even as Raf reached for her she began scrambling to the far side of the bed, intent on putting as much distance between them as possible.

'It's a bit too late for *no*,' he voiced with quiet savagery, trapping her within seconds and stilling her flailing arms with galling ease.

'Let me *go*, damn you!' she cried, sorely tried after trying to extricate herself from his grasp.

'Be quiet!' It was a husky admonition delivered close to her ear, and she groaned out loud as his mouth settled on a vulnerable pulse-beat in the hollow at the base of her neck and savoured its increased thudding tattoo.

Of their own volition her lips began to tremble. 'Damn you—*damn* you,' she whispered with impotent rage, hating him with a depth of feeling that was vaguely frightening.

Raf lifted his head and met her fiery gaze. 'Tell me you don't want me.' He lifted a hand and smoothed back the length of her hair in a strangely gentle gesture.

'I don't want you!'

For what seemed an age he simply looked at her, his eyes dark and unfathomable. Then he slowly released her and moved towards his discarded clothes, pulling on briefs and trousers before collecting his shirt and jacket and hooking them over one shoulder. Shoes, socks and tie were scooped together, and she watched as he walked to the door.

'Sweet dreams, Chelsea,' he said with dry cynicism, then he was gone, the almost silent click of the door as it closed behind him a subtle reminder that in punishing him she had also punished herself.

Now she was left in an empty void, her emotions shredded and her nerves tautened to their furthest limitation. Worst of all was the consuming ache that racked her body until it assumed a tangible pain.

With an angry movement she snatched up her silk wrap and slid into it, then she made her way into the adjoining bathroom, eyeing the shower and the adjacent spa-bath in turn before selecting the latter. Maybe the gentle pulsing jets would ease the build-up of sexual tension; perhaps disperse it—or at least lull her into a state of inertia where sleep was possible.

An hour later she lay in bed, deliciously perfumed from head to toe in her favourite Chanel, and about as close to blissful somnolence as a fractious baby.

Damn Raf! Damn him to hell. Yet what had she expected? *Rape*? That wasn't his style.

CHAPTER SEVEN

THE DAY began with a series of minor disasters, the first of which was the discovery of a ladder in a newly opened packet of tights; then Chelsea smudged her nail varnish. The outfit she wanted to wear to the office wasn't hanging in her wardrobe, and she belatedly remembered telling Hannah she'd collect it from the dry-cleaners, but she had completely forgotten because Raf's sudden reappearance in her life had swept such mundane details from her mind. Her Porsche, which for the past two years had maintained a flawless mechanical record, came to an unprecedented stop in the midst of heavy traffic and had to be towed away. There was no taxi in sight, and by the time she reached a telephone box, made the necessary call and waited for it to arrive, she was almost an hour late.

As if that wasn't enough. Susan had called in sick, and her temporary replacement bore every resemblance to a model from *Vogue*, which was fine if her secretarial skills matched her appearance, but they didn't, and files couldn't be found, messages magically disappeared and the mysteries of the internal telephone network proved a puzzling enigma.

By three o'clock Chelsea had had enough. She gave the girl the rest of the day off, organised a top-flight replacement from another agency, then rang Hannah to say she'd be late.

'Not too late, I hope. You haven't forgotten the Lumsdens' party this evening, preceded by cocktails with the Macquires?'

She had. Dammit, she was having Friday the thirteenth on Monday! Thank heaven it was only a matter of days until Christmas, for once the season's festivities were over she could look forward to a less hectic social existence.

'With a bit of luck I'll be home by five-thirty,' she said to herself and depressed the handset in preparation for another call.

'I'm sorry, Mrs Hamilton, but Mr Hamilton chartered a private flight to the Gold Coast this morning. Mr Prendergaast accompanied him.' The woman's voice assumed a puzzled tone. 'Mr Hamilton tried to get through to you early this morning, but you weren't in your office, and he particularly asked me to relay a message. Didn't you receive it?'

'No, I'm afraid not. Perhaps you'd better give it to me again.' Chelsea drummed her fingers against the edge of her desk and silently fumed as she learned that Raf wasn't expected in the office until the folowing morning.

The final straw came when the garage rang to say that the necessary part of her car wasn't available and would arrive by overnight courier from Melbourne the following day.

For the first time ever, she simply gathered up the files on her desk and locked them into her drawer without a shred of guilt, then she rang for a taxi and took the elevator down to the ground floor to await its arrival.

It was after six when she reached home, and she raced upstairs to shower and change in record time. The dress she'd selected at random was a bright crimson silk, figure-hugging to mid-thigh where the skirt frothed out from a bias-cut seam. The bodice was virtually strapless, except for twin shoestring straps that were an inclusion more for effect than actual support. With it she wore matching handmade shoes and carried a small, beaded evening purse. Her make-up was understated, except for her eyes, and she swept her hair high on top of her head, fastening it with a diamond clip. A diamond pendant and matching ear-rings completed the outfit, then a generous spray of perfume and she was ready.

Will was waiting downstairs with the Range Rover, and it wasn't until they had reached the Macquires' imposing Point Piper residence that Chelsea remembered Raf. Did he know about this evening's arrangement? A hollow laugh died in her throat. Unless he'd asked Hannah to check her social diary and inform him of all her upcoming engagements, he would be in total ignorance. Not that she cared a fig whether or not he put in an appearance, but in the light of their supposed reconciliation if would look rather odd if she went to both parties alone.

She stifled a silent curse, then gave a wry grimace. Cursing was becoming an increasing habit of late!

Well, there wasn't much she could do about it, other than leave a message with Will, and as most of the guests at the Macquire cocktail party were going on to the Lumsdens', it would be a simple matter to get a lift.

As with all parties in the upper social echelon, everything bore the appearance of refined affluence. Background music provided a pleasant intrusion, mingling with the constant buzz of conversation, and there was an abundance of tastefully prepared morsels of food to tempt the most critical palate, together with a wide variety of alcoholic beverages.

Chelsea felt her stomach protest in hunger, and realised it was with just cause. She hadn't stopped for lunch, and breakfast had been fresh orange juice, a slice of toast, and black coffee.

'All alone, darling?'

She turned and met the arched gaze of a well-known society matron whose avid glance assessed her dress, recognising its designer and approximate cost within seconds. 'Raf had to fly to the Coast,' Chelsea told her.

The eyebrow lifted even higher. 'But he'll be joining you, surely?'

'Oh, I hope so,' Chelsea responded sweetly. It was a question she was required to answer several times during the next few hours, and at the Lumsdens' it became clearly apparent that Raf's absence was causing considerable speculation.

'You're looking extremely thoughtful.'

She turned to meet the dark, gleaming gaze of the man standing within touching distance and offered him a brilliant smile.

'Raf! How nice that you could make it.'

Sardonic cynicism flared briefly, and his mouth formed a mocking twist. 'So considerate of you to have told me you were attending two parties this evening.' An eyebrow slanted in quizzical query, and she was unable to prevent the faint quickening of her pulse.

'You'd already left by the time I came down for breakfast. And for the record, I'd forgotten all about both of them until Hannah reminded me.' What was the use in trying to explain that she had tried to contact him, albeit without success? It was maddening, but she felt quite light-headed, almost as if she'd imbibed too much alcohol, and yet she hadn't had more than one glass all evening.

His gaze became assessing and vaguely analytical. 'I left a message with your secretary as to my whereabouts.'

A weary sigh left her lips. 'I never received it. Susan called in sick, and anything that could go wrong, did.'

'So it would appear.'

His dry cynicism was the living end. 'Anyone would think I deliberately engineered my car's mechanical fault, personally delivered a contagious virus to Susan's doorstep and hired an empty-headed Barbie doll to fill her place!' Now that she'd started, she couldn't stop. '*You*, of course, would be able to manufacture out of thin air an elusive motor-part that in the normal course of events is available in Sydney, but had to be couriered from Melbourne, enlist the services of a super-secretary, and continue to function with one hand tied behind your back!'

'Careful, darling, your claws are showing.'

'Don't call me that!' Her mouth bore a generous curve, even her eyes were wide and suitably adoring, but her voice was sufficiently low to ensure it couldn't be overheard.

'Darling?' Raf reached out and removed a glass of champagne from the tray of a hovering waiter. 'Why ever not?' One eyebrow slanted quizzically above eyes that held a gleam of amusement.

'Because,' she enunciated carefully, 'it's totally unnecessary.'

'You think so?'

'Yes!' Anger seemed to be her only weapon, and she nearly died when he leant forward and brushed his lips close to her ear.

'We're supposed to be a loving couple, remember?'

'*Supposed* being the operative word.'

His gaze narrowed and assumed an inscrutability, a watchfulness that was distinctly dangerous. 'That can be rectified at any time.'

Why did she suddenly feel an uncontrollable urge to lash out and hit him? Yet conversely, somewhere deep inside there was a strange reckless sensation that had liquid passion as its base, a soul-destroying *need* for a total satiation of the senses. Perhaps she should indulge the dictates of her flesh and forget everthing else. The knowledge of just how easy it would be to succumb sent a frisson of fearful anticipation spiralling through her body, and for a few seconds she actually considered initiating it.

As damnable as it was for her, it was a hundred times worse to discover that he *knew*, for she glimpsed the recognition in the depths of his eyes, the curious tenseness at the edge of his jaw—and hated him for it.

'Raf, *darling*.' The emphasis was delicately deliberate. 'Five days without a willing female in your bed must be proving absolute hell!' Chelsea even managed an incredibly sweet and sympathetic smile. 'I remember you were always such a sexually *hungry* man.'

For one infinitesimal second his eyes leapt with icy anger, then he calmly reached out a hand and curled his fingers round her nape, then lowered his head to within inches of her own.

'Don't you *dare*!' Chelsea hissed, hopelessly trapped and unable to struggle without causing a scene. She was powerless to do anything but stand helplessly still as his mouth closed over hers, his lips silkily soft, seductive in a manner that sent a frisson of fear spiralling through her body.

Then it was over, and she let her lashes sweep down to form a protective veil, aware of an acute feeling of isolation knowing that the kiss had been witnessed by at least half of the guests present in the large lounge.

'Where are our hosts? We should at least thank them for their invitation before we make our farewells.'

For a moment she found it difficult to assimilate his words, then realisation dawned, and with it came searing rage. 'We can't leave yet!'

'My dear Chelsea, of course we can,' Raf returned easily. 'And don't come back at me with the classic query of "what will people think?" ' His smile was vaguely cruel beneath its pleasant veneer. 'I imagine it will be patently obvious why we're leaving.'

'They'll be wrong.'

'Will they?' With icy calm he put his glass, then hers, on to a nearby table.

There was nothing she could do about his steel-like grasp on her elbow, and short of effecting an undignified struggle she had little choice but to walk at his side as he found Lloyd and Pattie Lumsden and made their excuses.

The instant they reached the Jaguar, Chelsea attempted in vain to break loose from his hold. 'How dare you?' Even in the dim street lighting she could glimpse the grim purpose evident as he unlocked the passenger door.

'Get in the car, Chelsea.'

'What if I refuse?'

'Perversity simply for the sheer hell of it? Unwise, wouldn't you say?'

'Perhaps,' she declared vengefully.

'I suggest we go home and argue, rather than conduct a shouting match in the middle of the street.'

He was right, but it didn't make it any easier for her to capitulate, and she slid mutinously into the front seat to sit staring straight ahead as he crossed round the bonnet to the car and slipped in behind the wheel.

Even when the car was in motion she didn't offer so much as a word, choosing instead to focus her attention beyond the windscreen, although the clear blue-black sky with its sprinkling of stars escaped her, as did the slim sickle moon. Instead, she stared sightlessly at the reflected glow of street lights, the glimpses of houses behind a variety of protective walls, fences and shrubbery.

Within what seemed a very short space of time the Jaguar swung into their curved driveway and slid to a halt inside the garage.

The silence was almost cataclysmic, and Chelsea sat frozen into immobility for all of ten seconds before sanity demanded action, motivating her limbs into co-ordinating movement as she reached for the door-clasp and slid out from the car.

Raf was behind her, a potent, engulfing force, so much so that she could almost feel him as he followed her into the house. Without even hesitating she moved towards the staircase, mounting the carpeted treads with controlled deliberation, when every instinct screamed for her to run as fast as she could.

Her bedroom was at the end of the hallway, and she had almost reached it when a hand closed over her shoulder, halting her progress.

'In here, I think,' Raf insisted as he leaned forward and opened the door leading to their shared sitting-room.

'I have nothing whatsoever to say to you,' Chelsea declared, turning to face him as she reached the middle of the room, aware of two factors simultaneously, the soft, controlled clunk of the door closing behind him and his hard, inflexible expression, each of which had a shattering effect on her nerves.

'Indeed? You had no such reservations surrounded by guests at the Lumsdens' party.'

She looked at him warily, unsure precisely what he intended. 'I'm tired. I want to go to bed.'

'So you shall—eventually.'

He was standing far too close for her peace of mind, and a defiant sparkle lit her eyes. 'Oh, I see. I'm to be punished for daring to speak the truth.'

'Which particular aspect of it are you referring to?'

'Take your pick. I really don't care.'

Raf regarded her silently for what seemed an age, and she felt as if each separate pulse-beat quickened until together they reached a deafening, unifying tattoo.

Slowly he reached out a hand and touched a finger against the thudding pulse at the hollow of her throat, and she flinched as if burned by flame.

'Don't!' The single word emerged as an anguished cry, and he smiled faintly.

'Don't—*what*?' His finger slid slowly upward until it rested against the edge of her mouth.

'Leave me alone!' It was a cry from the heart, and she felt incredibly afraid he intended to disregard it.

'Why, Chelsea? On a physical level we were always in perfect accord.' His eyes darkened fractionally as his head lowered towards hers. 'I retain a vivid recollection that it was our one salvation.'

Even as she began a protest, it was stilled beneath the hungry, ravaging possession of his mouth. Any attempt to struggle proved fruitless, and a silent groan of self-defeat rose and died in her throat as frustrated, angry tears clouded her vision.

Futility fanned a deep inner rage, and she railed her fists against his shoulders, his back, his ribs—anywhere she could reach, until blazing resentment forced her to resort to damnable revenge. Even as she brought her teeth together she felt the sudden stillness in his body, then her mouth was freed and his husky oath was viciously explicit.

Her eyes became locked with his, dilating, unblinking, expressive, as time paused in explosive suspension, and she was unprepared for the unleashed strength of his powerful body as his fingers slid with careless disregard through her hair, loosening it from the clips that held the upswept style in place.

She couldn't move, her body was so successfully bound against his own that it was even difficult to breathe, and she cried out in anguish as his mouth plundered her own at will, his probing tongue demandingly insistent as he heartlessly pressured her soft lips against her teeth, allowing her no licence to repeat any revenge, for her jaw ached beneath his invasion, its strength harnessed and hopelessly out-matched by his own.

As a punishment it was very effective, and she drew in deep, ragged gulps of air as his mouth slid down the slender column of her throat, then lower to the slim cleft that separated her breasts.

'No—don't!' The words escaped as a tortured groan, then subsided into husky torment as his finger deftly slid down the zip of her dress and assisted it over her slim curves to slither to the carpet. 'You can't!'

Her only undergarment was soft satin French-styled briefs, for the dress was boned, lined, and designed to be worn without the benefit of bra or slip.

Raf took his fill just looking at the perfection of her rose-tipped breasts, the slim, curved waist, and the slender length of her legs. Her skin seemed to burn as each blood vessel became engorged with re-membrance of the passionate fire his touch could evoke, and she was powerless to prevent the delicately pale blush that crept over her body.

A terrible sense of defeat began to destroy her urge to continue this wretched one-sided fight. What did she have to lose except her own stupid pride? *Self-respect*, a tiny voice taunted. What about that? Don't you care that you'll have none left when you wake tomorrow?

Without taking his eyes from her face Raf slowly began to undress, removing every last vestige of his clothing, then he slid an arm beneath her knees and effortlessly lifted her into his arms.

'No!' Why had she simply stood there, mesmerised, when she could have turned and run?

'There's a limit to my tolerance, and tonight you've overreached it,' he declared with chilling determination as he walked towards her bedroom, opening the door with one hand, then sending it shut with a forceful kick.

'You can't do this to me!' Chelsea cried as he let her slide down to stand in front of him.

'Permit you to tease and provoke, then retreat?' His gaze was startlingly direct, and utterly merciless. 'For how long, Chelsea? Until you tire of the game? Or is this what you wanted all along? A wild, savage slaking of physical pleasure?' He let his eyes rove over every visible inch of delectable flesh before coming to rest on her mouth. 'Stop me,' he added with ungentle mockery as he cupped one breast and teased it into pulsing life, while his other hand slid down to caress her hip. 'If you can.'

She moved restlessly, willing her body not to respond to his flagrant seduction, hating the way he could make her feel, and she began to fight, hitting out at him in the only way she knew how until she fell backwards on to the bed, propelled there by one easy thrust. Before she could scramble away, he joined her, trapping her slim legs with one of his own, stilling her flailing arms and holding them together above her head without any effort at all.

'Let me *go*!' Her plea was a low, guttural demand that was met with ruthless disregard as his mouth lowered towards her breast.

'Where can you escape to? Another room? The hallway, perhaps, before I caught up with you?' His soft laugh was entirely mirthless. 'Oh, no, Chelsea. This,' he paused as his lips sought the soft swell, then lingered over the hard, thrusting peak, caressing it into renewed life with the roughness of his tongue, '*this* is inevitable.'

'It isn't, damn you! *It isn't!*' Even as the deep, sobbing denial was torn from her lips, her body began its own traitorous dance as each sensory centre throbbed into awareness. Raf was totally merciless, wreaking havoc as his lips brushed a treacherous path as they traversed every hollow, each moist crevice, until she cried out for his possession and the relief it would provide from this tormented, aching passion that had its roots in primitive, primeval desire. She threshed beneath him, almost beyond reason as he effected consummation with one powerful thrust, and she cried out his name as he began a slow, sure pacing, driving deep into the yielding, silken flesh until he was unable to withhold control any longer.

Afterwards she lay still, languorous and filled with an aching warmth. She felt—oh, dear heaven, *how* did she feel? Fulfilled, satiated? *Yes*, in a purely physical sense, but emotionally she wasn't exactly wildly happy. After Raf? Now that the challenge of getting her into his bed—*her* bed, she corrected wryly—

had been met, would he mark her off his mythical list of achievements?

A butterfly touch at her temple brought her eyes wide open, and she turned her head slightly towards him, seeing the faint frown evident, the deep, sleepy warmth of his eyes as they swept her features in keen appraisal.

'I think I'll take a shower.' Chelsea said the words quietly, wanting to move away from him, yet contrarily wanting to stay. Yet she couldn't just lie there, trying to make believe what had happened between them was a figment of her imagination. Two years ago—no, almost three—he would have curved her close against him and pillowed her head on his shoulder, kissed her tenderly, and made her feel the most infinitely precious female alive.

Slipping off the bed, she walked through to the bathroom and carefully closed the door, then she turned and moved to turn on the shower, changed her mind and filled the spa-bath instead. Adding essence, she wound her hair into a knot and fixed it with pins on top of her head, then she stopped, arrested by the slim silhouette reflected in the wide mirror. She looked—different, somehow. Her skin was faintly pink in places were Raf had kissed her, and there were slight bruises on her upper arms from when she'd struggled against him.

Steam from the bath began to mist the mirror, and she turned off the taps, switched on the jets, then stepped into the gently pulsing water. She had just picked up the soap when the door swung open, and her eyes widened as Raf entered the bathroom and calmly stepped into the bath behind her.

'What do you think you're doing?' Even to her own ears her voice sounded incredulous, bordering on scandalised hysteria as he took the soap from her nerveless fingers.

'Enjoying the pleasure of bathing you.'

'I'm quite capable of doing it myself!' She attempted to snatch the soap from his hand and failed.

'So you are,' he soothed, gently running the soap down her arm. 'Just relax.'

The softness of his voice had a hypnotic effect, and besides, she didn't really have the energy to fight him. Slowly she let her eyelids flicker down, and sat perfectly still as he soaped her skin with a seductive touch so exquisite that she was damnably aware of her body's response as the fingers of one hand trailed an evocative path while the other used the soap to cleanse. She could feel his lips caress her nape, then follow the gentle slope from her neck down to the tip of her shoulder.

She had little conception of how long they stayed there, for she experienced no realisation of the passage of time, just a dreamy sense of inertia related to the aftermath of lovemaking; the promise that it hadn't really stopped.

Chelsea didn't demur as Raf switched off the jets, then released the water, and she let him pull her from the bath, then towel her dry—even dust her skin with Chanel talc, before removing the moisture from his own body. Then he led her into the bedroom and gently tugged her down on to the bed and into his arms, where he proceeded to make love to her all over again with such infinite delicacy that she transcended mere sensation and floated higher, into a world of sensual ecstasy so fraught with eroticism that she never wanted it to end.

CHAPTER EIGHT

CHELSEA must have slept, for when she woke the fingers of a new day's dawn were filtering through the curtains. In the same instant, as her eyes adjusted to the dimly lit room, she became aware of an arm lying heavily across her waist, a long, muscular leg successfully trapping her own. Carefully she turned her head on the pillow and saw that Raf's features were still relaxed in sleep. His dark hair was ruffled, his piercing grey eyes shuttered, lending an air of vulnerability she found fascinating. The sheet lay tangled in complete disarray, providing inadequate covering, and her eyes travelled to his broad chest, taking in the dark whorls of hair, the exposed length of his legs, before slowly trailing back to his face, and a pair of gleaming eyes watchfully intent as she completed her inspection.

'Good morning.' His smile was warm and intimate and infinitely lazy. Rising up on one elbow, he looked down at her and idly traced his finger across the tender curves of her lips, the tip of her nose, before slipping slowly to the cleft between her breasts.

'Raf——'

'Hmm?' His mouth hovered above her own, then descended in a kiss that made her feel as if she was melting into a thousand pieces.

Her whole body seemed consumed by one large ache; an ache that had everything to do with prolonged celibacy, she recognised wryly. Little-used muscles promised to make their presence felt if she moved so much as an inch, and she lifted her hands to cup his head, letting her fingers thread through the dark hair that grew back from his temples.

'Please, I must get up.' A treacherous weakness invaded her limbs, and if she didn't make a positive effort to get out of bed she'd be lost in the magical, elusive alchemy that seemed to enshroud them both.

'Must?' He sounded genuinely regretful, and she wrinkled her nose at him in bewitching humour.

'Yes,' she said decidedly, and slipped out of his embrace. 'I'm going to have a shower, walk the dogs eat breakfast, read the morning paper, then drive to work.'

'All of which will take an hour,' he teased as he rolled on to his back and crossed his arms behind his head, his eyes alive with passionate warmth as they viewed her progress across the room.

'Two,' Chelsea retorted equably as she went into the bathroom and closed the door behind her.

It was going to be another hot, humid day, with temperatures promising to reach the high thirties, she thought as she unclipped the leashes used to restrain Ming and Pasha on their morning walk. Even at this relatively early hour there was a burning heat in the sun's reflected rays.

'Inside, both of you,' she instructed, smiling as the two little dogs leapt forward and chased each other into the kitchen for a much-needed drink, while she followed at a more leisurely pace.

'I'll serve breakfast on the terrace,' Hannah decided as she deftly slid eggs and bacon on to a pre-heated plate. 'Will has organised the caterers for tonight, and the hired help will arrive mid-afternoon.'

A perplexed frown creased Chelsea's forehead, then realisation dawned. The party! She'd forgotten all about it.

'I must say it will be nice to see people in the house again,' Hannah continued. 'Your father loved to entertain.'

Sam had certainly adored the social circuit, the giving of parties and attending them. The house had been alive with guests almost every weekend, Chelsea reflected. A vast difference from the past two years when she'd chosen to keep a low profile, apart from a few special occasions, when she'd preferred to invite trusted friends and business associates to dinner rather than indulge in glittering parties.

'I'll ensure I get away from the office by three,' Chelsea said as she took a glass and filled it with orange juice. 'That will give me plenty of time to check with you on last-minute details.'

'Wonderful if you can, although Raf has made all the arrangements and seen that ample staff have been hired to help out.' Hannah's eyes glowed. 'I'm really looking forward to it.'

I wish I was, Chelsea thought silently as she followed Hannah out on to the terrace where Raf was seated at the table, seemingly engrossed in the *Financial Times*.

He glanced up as they approached, his eyes

conducting an appreciative, gleaming appraisal of the brief satin shorts, sleeveless top and trainers she'd worn to walk the dogs.

Chelsea took a seat opposite and ate one piece of toast while Raf did justice to his cooked meal, and after two cups of coffee she excused herself on the pretext of going upstairs to get ready for work.

She felt hot after walking almost two kilometres with Ming and Pasha, and she elected to take a quick shower before changing into a pencil-slim grey skirt and cream silk blouse. Black accessories added an elegant contrast, and after skilfully applying her make-up and styling her hair she collected her briefcase and made her way to the foyer where Raf stood waiting.

'Ready?'

Chelsea nodded in silent acquiescence, and in the car she couldn't think of a single thing to say that wouldn't come out sounding contrived or inane. The safest topic of conversation seemed to be this evening's party, and she ran the entire gamut of questions from the number of guests expected to attend to precisely *who*, feeling immensely relieved when the Jaguar pulled into its parking bay beneath the city building.

'I'll check with the garage about your car,' Raf told her as they took the lift to the thirty-first floor.

'Thanks. I'd like to leave early.'

'Otherwise take mine, and I'll drive the Porsche home.'

The elevator doors opened and they walked into the Houghton-Hamilton foyer, bade the receptionist 'good morning', then made their way to their respective offices.

Susan was still absent, but her temporary replacement looked coolly efficient—so much so that Chelsea had no qualms about dictating a pile of correspondence, then taking an extended lunch break. To purchase, she decided, something new and sensational to wear for this evening's party.

She found it in a ruinously expensive boutique: an electric-blue silk taffeta with a ruched bodice, a fitted skirt, and an off-the-shoulder neckline. There were matching slim-heeled shoes, and she didn't even blink at the price-tag as she charged it to her account.

When she arrived back at the office there was a set of keys to the Jaguar resting on her desk, and a message from Raf that her Porsche would be ready late that afternoon. After checking and signing the completed correspondence, she asked her secretary to let Raf know she was on her way home, then she collected her packages, scooped up the car keys and made her way towards the elevator.

The house was a veritable hive of activity when Chelsea eased the Jaguar past three vans parked on the crest of the driveway. Two bore the recognised insignia of an exclusive catering firm, while the third belonged to the local florist.

After checking with Hannah, she fetched a glass of chilled fruit juice and retired out on to the terrace to run through the guest list, her eyes widening at three notable inclusions—Krysia, whom she had partly expected, but Paula and David Vennables normally resided in Los Angeles. Brother and sister, and immensely wealthy, they ran a very successful agency which had links in several capital cities around the world. Their reason for visiting Australia, particularly Sydney, within days of Raf's re-appearance on these Antipodean shores, seemed far too coincidental for Chelsea's peace of mind.

It niggled away at the back of her brain for the remainder of the afternoon, and during dinner she was so incredibly polite that it gained her a teasing lift of one expressive eyebrow as Raf queried, 'Something bothering you, Chelsea?'

'Why should you think that?'

'I recognise the signs.'

His vaguely dry tones ignited a spark of latent anger. 'Really?' You must possess the most remarkable memory.'

'Oh, but I do,' he returned silkily, and she experienced a feeling of acute vulnerability.

Was she that transparent? She hoped not. It gave her an eerie sensation to even think he could see through the windows of her mind to the depths of her soul. It wasn't remotely fair when *he* was an unfathomable enigma she couldn't begin to understand.

With a gesture of indifference she pushed her plate aside, her appetite lost. Not that it had been very robust to begin with, for she was consumed with nervous tension. Added to which was an inner weariness and lack of sleep that would require tremendous effort to overcome in order to summon sufficient *savoir-faire* with which to play the part of sparkling hostess.

'If you'll excuse me, I'll go and get ready.' She spared her watch a quick glance. 'Our guests will begin arriving in an hour.'

Upstairs she quickly showered and washed her hair, then, towelled dry, she liberally applied her favourite body lotion, added matching talc, then stepped into fresh underwear. Her hair came next, and she blowdried it, then arranged it into an elaborate pleat. Make-up was carefully and skilfully applied, highlighting her eyes, her mouth, with a touch of blusher to give her cheeks some colour.

Tights, sheer and an opalescent shimmery blue, were the perfect foil for her shoes, and she stepped into her dress and slid the fastener into position before standing back to view her overall reflection in the cheval mirror.

'Beautiful,' drawled Raf from the connecting doorway, and Chelsea turned slightly as he moved towards her, a pair of cufflinks held in one hand.

He looked arresting, his black trousers hugging slim hips and long, muscular thighs, his white dress-shirt buttoned almost to the neck with a black bow-tie lying undone beneath the collar.

'Fix these for me, will you?'

Dynamic, Chelsea thought silently as he stood in front of her. His aftershave teased her nostrils, musky and evocative, and this close it was all too easy to be intimidated by his strength, the intense passion she knew to exist beneath the surface of his control.

'How have you managed in the past?' she queried, and heard his faint, husky laugh.

'I didn't think you'd object to performing a minor wifely chore.'

Her fingers felt clumsy, although outwardly she managed to slip the keepers into place without too much effort, then she stood back feeling vastly unsure of her ability to remain calm as Raf motioned to his tie. Without a word she fastened the elastic clip, then slid the bow into position.

She was powerless to elude his touch as he took hold of her chin, and she glimpsed the dark, glittery expression in the depths of his eyes before she lowered her lashes.

'You have an enchanting air of fragility, a bruised quality that frightens me,' he told her broodingly, and her eyelids flickered upwards to reveal sparkling green fire.

'I *am* bruised,' she retorted. 'Inside and out.' But it was her heart that was breaking, and the pain became more unbearable with every passing minute.

'Poor *querida*! Love can be absolute hell, can't it?'

Every vestige of colour drained from her face for a few terrible seconds until she regained her composure, and she missed the faint narrowing of his eyes, the small muscle that momentarily tensed the edge of his jaw.

She stood transfixed as his lips sought the delicately perfumed curve of her neck, then she was free, and he caught hold of her hand, tugging it gently as he moved towards the connecting door.

'Come with me while I get my jacket, then we'll go downstairs together.'

It was a splendidly successful party, Alyse complimented with sincere enthusiasm within an hour of arriving, and Chelsea began to relax as she saw the mingling guests giving every appearance of enjoying themselves. The hired staff circulated with professional ease, proffering trays of tastefully prepared food and fresh glasses of champagne.

It was, without doubt, a replay of any one of the numerous parties Sam had hosted over the years, and Chelsea suppressed a strange, shivery sensation in the knowledge that it would take little imagination to believe her father was actually here.

'Cold?'

She tilted her head and met Raf's faintly narrowed gaze.

'No.' She even managed a slight winsome smile. 'A ghost just walked over my grave.'

'Sam?' His mouth quirked slightly, although his eyes were remarkably solemn. 'I think he would have approved, don't you?'

There was no other answer to give, except *yes*, and if she felt transported back in time that was her problem and hers alone.

'Why, Raf—*Chelsea*. Sorry we're late, but the hotel restaurant took ages to serve our meal, and then I couldn't decide what to wear. And, my dears, absolutely every cab in Sydney was engaged, I swear. We waited *hours* for one to arrive!'

Paula. Tall, svelte, and incredibly soignée, dressed by Yves St Laurent, shod by Charles Jourdan, and perfumed by Dior.

She looked a million dollars, and was probably wearing it in jewellery alone, Chelsea decided, making a valiant effort to be charitable as she summoned a truly stunning smile.

'Chelsea, darling—so delightful to see you again!'

David. Impeccably suited and handsomely groomed, he was incredibly brilliant with anything related to business, but terribly bored by everything else.

'Raf, one can't possibly imagine you staying long in this Colonial outpost,' purred Paula, placing her exquisitely long, lacquered nails on his arm. 'When can we except you back in Los Angeles?'

Chelsea stood perfectly still in mesmerised fascination as she watched Raf deliberately remove Paula's hand.

'That's an answer I can't provide at the moment,' he said silkily.

'Why should he?' David offered with studied indifference.

'Chelsea, darling, do show me the powder-room—I think I have an eyelash in my eye.'

For a brief second Chelsea hesitated, then she almost died as Raf caught hold of her hand and lifted it to his lips, blatantly kissing each separate finger with lingering warmth.

'Ask any one of the staff, Paula,' he drawled. 'They'll be only too helpful in directing you to it.'

His gaze didn't falter from Chelsea's face, and she looked momentarily stricken, torn between rage and the need to know why he was conducting such a flagrant seduction in full view of everyone.

'But surely Chelsea ——'

'*No*, Paula,' he said softly.

Hard eyes locked with his, and Chelsea held her breath as Paula's beautifully classic features assumed an icy hauteur. 'I see.'

'Do you, Paula? I very much hope so. For your sake,' Raf added with deadly ruthlessness.

'Just one thing, darling,' Paula arched with apparent carelessness. 'Why give me an invitation to your party?'

'David is one of my valued associates, and has been for several years. Quite why he's in Sydney at this particular time, I'm unsure, although I suspect you precipitated his visit. When he rang yesterday, I suggested you both might like to join us this evening.' Raf paused, then added with chilling finality, 'To celebrate my reconciliation with my wife.'

'Good heavens, that has such a solid ring to it! One wonders how long this so-called reconciliation will last.'

'So-called? Are you suggesting it's contrived? I can assure you Chelsea shares my bed, Paula.'

'Yes, now that I look closely, she does appear rather tired. But then, darling, the woman who takes you on requires—' Paula paused, then added delicately, 'stamina. Perhaps she simply isn't able to stand the pace?'

'Paula, my sweet,' David intervened, 'you're a, bitch. A beautiful, clever bitch, but a bitch, none the less. Put down your drink and come with me while I find someone to call us a cab. I think too highly of Raf to allow you to stay a minute longer.'

Chelsea stood quite still, her features momentarily frozen. She was entirely familiar with the vagaries of the socially élite, the bitchiness and one-upmanship, the games certain women played out of sheer boredom. And men. It was the main reason she'd opted out of the social scene when she left the States, and Raf. At times during the first year of her marriage, it had seemed as if she'd merely exchanged one social scene for another; different countries, but the ambience was exactly the same. Although she had to admit that Paula Vennables took top marks for being the most persistent woman she'd ever met. Within days of Chelsea and Raf returning from their honeymoon in Paris, Paula had made her presence felt, always at the same parties, the same functions, her skilfully inflicted poison insidious enough to cast doubts in Chelsea's mind.

'I'll get you a drink.'

Chelsea barely registered Raf's voice, and when he put a fresh glass in her hand she obediently sipped at its contents, slowly feeling the numbness subside.

How many people had witnessed that vicious altercation? Probably at least half of those present, Chelsea decided, although it was doubtful anyone had actually overheard what had transpired.

Somehow she managed to get through the rest of the evening projecting a vivacity that was totally contrived. She determinedly smiled so often that her face felt as if it would crack by the time the last few remaining guests floated towards the front door amid apparently genuine platitudes in compliment of having enjoyed a wonderful party.

As soon as the front door closed behind them, Chelsea visibly relaxed, the forced effervescent mask slipping away as she turned towards the man at her side.

'Everyone enjoyed themselves, don't you think?'

'Indeed. You, however, did not.'

She cast him a startled glance. 'Was it obvious?'

'Only to me.'

There seemed to be a curious lump in her throat, and her limbs suddenly felt incapable of any movement.

'Go on up to bed, Chelsea. 'I'll check with Hannah and Will.'

Without a word she turned and walked towards the stairs, and in her bedroom she slowly removed her clothes, then her make-up, before slipping into her nightgown. Now there was only her hair, and she pulled out the pins, then brushed its length, feeling it crackle and spring into life to cloud round her features like a spun-gold nimbus.

She should have felt tired, but instead her nerves seemed stretched beyond endurance, and her emotions were in such a state of conflict that she couldn't think clearly.

A slight sound alerted her attention, and she swung round to see that Raf had entered the room. His expression was unfathomable, and one glance was sufficient for the nerves in her stomach to begin an agonising somersault.

Anger seemed to be her only weapon, and she used it shamelessly. 'What do you think you're doing here?'

He moved towards her with slow, lithe ease, his jacket hooked over one shoulder. 'Your room or mine. It doesn't matter which.'

Chelsea closed her eyes against the compelling sight of him, then slowly opened them again. 'No'.

'*Yes*,' he insisted with dangerous softness.

'Last night——'

'Was a mere transgression?' Raf intervened, his features assuming wry cynicism. 'Oh, no, Chelsea, you don't believe that, any more than I do.'

'So what happens now?' Her eyes were stormy as she glared at him. 'Am I supposed to slip back into the marriage bed and pretend the past few years never happened?'

He tossed his jacket down on to a nearby chair, then began discarding his clothes. When he returned for the belt on his trousers Chelsea simply turned on her heel and walked towards the connecting door. If he intended staying in her room, she'd sleep in *his* bed!

Her fierce independence didn't do her the slightest bit of good, of course, for in less than a minute he followed her, and she stood still, her eyes wary as she watched him close the distance between them.

'Can't you see I'm tired?' There was an angry desperation in her voice that wasn't contrived. She didn't possess the strength to fight him on a physical level, at least not tonight. 'Even Paula chose to comment on it.'

Raf's expression didn't alter. 'Paula, as David so aptly remarked, is a beautiful, clever bitch.'

And incredibibly dangerous, Chelsea added silently, her eyes widening and filling with an aching intensity as Raf lifted a hand and idly brushed his fingers down her cheek.

'Don't. Please,' she whispered. 'I don't think I could bear it.'

His eyes kindled with something she couldn't define. 'Share my bed, Chelsea,' he said gently. 'I give my word that I'll only hold you. Nothing more.'

The thought of being cradled in his arms was tempting, and she closed her eyes against the prick of painful tears as he caught her up into his arms and laid her between the sheets before joining her in the large bed.

His body was warm, and strong, she didn't protest when he pillowed her head against his shoulder, nor did she move when one hand slid to her breast and the other rested on her hip. She could feel his breath stir the tendrils of hair at her temple, and slowly, physically and mentally, she began to relax.

She slept, with dreams chasing her subconscious mind, sweet, sad dreams that made her want to weep and brought her into wakefulness, feeling poignantly bereft for a few heartstopping seconds until realisation of where she was and with whom gradually permeated her mind. For a long while she lay perfectly still, listening to Raf's even breathing, hearing the strong beat of his heart beneath her cheek, then with infinite care she slowly shifted the arm lying across her hip and slid out from the bed.

The connecting door stood open, and she moved through to the sitting-room to stand at the window looking out over the swimming pool to the perfect stillness of the garden bathed in an early pre-dawn light.

She stirred slightly as the sky began to lighten, watching in idle fascination as it changed from dark grey to silver; then the shadows began to shift and change dimension as everything before her eyes assumed its natural colour. And there was life, birds fluttered to the ground in search of food, chirruping their pleasure, and she saw Sheikh execute an early-morning round of the grounds, pausing here and there to sniff the air, nuzzle the roots of a shrub, then break into a loose-limbed lollop for a few metres before slowing down to explore something else that caught his attention.

The crystal-clear depths of the pool looked inviting, and she moved towards her own room, quickly slipping out of her nightgown and into a slinky black maillot. Then she caught up a towel and moved quickly and quietly downstairs.

She unlocked the back door, greeted Ming and Pasha, then Sheikh, before crossing the terrace to the steps that led down to the pool. Once there, she discarded the towel and executed a neat dive into the cool depths, emerging to stroke several lengths before pausing midway and idly turning on to her back to float aimlessly until a faint splash alerted her attention, and seconds later a dark head rose out of the water, close beside her.

'Good morning.'

'Hi.' Chelsea tried to sound cool, and failed miserably, unable to do a thing as Raf captured her face between his hands and bestowed a long, lingering kiss on her lips.

The instant he released her she propelled herself away from him, feeling a faint flush colour her cheeks as she heard his deep chuckle. To her chagrin, he calmly adjusted his stroking pace to her own, until she stood near the steps and retreated from the pool.

'Black coffee would go down well,' Raf commented as he followed her and removed the excess moisture from his tall frame with his towel.

Chelsea felt the breath catch in her throat just looking at him. 'I'll take a shower and get dressed first.'

'Good idea.'

She was supremely conscious of him as he walked at her side into the house and up the stairs. As she went into her bedroom he was close behind, and she felt a strange shivery sensation pervade her body as she turned towards him.

'Raf——'

His expression was deliberately bland. 'What, Chelsea? Get out of my room? Don't touch me?'

Hurt clouded her eyes, and she glanced away, unsure whether the sheer futility of how she felt about him would ever be resolved.

'Look at me.' When she didn't, he took hold of her chin and turned her face towards him. 'What were you going to say?'

Dear heaven, where did they go from here? Another argument? More anger? She knew she would be unable to bear it.

'I think we should talk.' There, she'd actually said it. Slowly she let her eyes widen, their depths solemn and unwavering as they met his.

There was a curious stillness in his stance, a waiting quality that was almost frightening. 'I'm listening.'

Maybe, just maybe, it was time for total honesty. Two years ago Chelsea had been too bitter to do anything but escape. Now she had reached a point where to continue fighting him would only result in destruction—*hers*.

'I'm not sure where to start.' It was ridiculous, but she felt as if she had suddenly fallen off the edge of a cliff and was free-falling down through space.

'Why not at the beginning?'

Where precisely was that? When she had first met him; their marriage; or when things started to go wrong?

'Perhaps if Sam had taken me into his confidence,

told me of his intention and *why*, I might have been more—philosophical.' She raised her chin a fraction and met Raf's steadfast gaze, holding it with a mixture of courage, pride, and innate dignity. 'It was shattering to discover our marriage was——' she paused, hesitant in search of an appropriate word, 'arranged.' Her eyes darkened, their depths clouding with remembered pain. Yet, now that she had started, there could be no retraction, no going back. 'Devastating to learn that it was common knowledge and a source of social gossip. I felt like a wife whose husband was having an affair—the last to know.' Amazing, she could even summon a shaky, mirthless smile.

'Despite the social merry-go-round my father maintained, my existence was a sheltered one. From choice,' she added quietly. 'I'd spent a lifetime watching a variety of socialites carrying out number-less ploys in their pursuit of idle entertainment—the ensnarement of the opposite sex, the inescapable intrigue of gossip.' Her lips twisted in a faint *moue* of distaste. 'It was all a fascinating game in which only the skilled players survived.' Somehow she managed to dredge up a smile, a poor imitation tinged with incredible sadness. 'And you were very skilled, Raf. I never guessed that our marriage was a sham—not once. Like a gullible fool I fell prey to every gesture of affection you bestowed on me. The fact that Sam held you in such high regard made it all seem like a dream come true.'

She glimpsed a faint tightening of muscle at the edge of his jaw, yet his eyes remained dark and unfathomable. Remorse? She thought not.

'You allowed me no room for doubt, did you, Raf? No time. You swept me off my feet, slid a ring on my finger, and put me on the roller-coaster that was your life-style.' She lifted her hand in a self-deprecatory gesture, then let it slip back to her side. 'Falling in love for the first time is a devastating experience. You give everything of yourself—heart and soul, with no holding back. During those first few months of our marriage I soared like a bird in a garden of paradise, ecstatically happy, as I'd never been before.' She paused to swallow the faint lump that had risen in her throat, the memory hauntingly vivid, even now, of what was to come, and she chose her words with care, aware that perhaps with their uttering she might effect some form of exorcism. A cleansing that might somehow create a miracle.

'But in nature's garden there's always a touch of ugliness to balance the beauty, and in mine there were a few serpents only too ready to compete with each other in their attempt to destroy me. At first, I didn't listen to their voiced innuendo. I was able to convince myself that I had no right to censure any of your numerous affairs that had occurred before our marriage. But the gossip was incredibly damaging, and they made sure it was supplemented with proof. Delighting, I think, in extending luncheon invitations of which at least one of your former——' Chelsea paused, enunciating delicately, 'bedmates were included.'

For a moment she thought Raf was about to intervene, and she waited, almost willing him to express some form of denial, but it wasn't forthcoming.

'I become increasingly vulnerable, insecure and doubtful. You had only to be late home to dinner for me to become suspicious, and with the suspicion came anger—at you, but mostly with myself for not having the courage to force a confrontation.' She took a deep breath and continued, 'I became withdrawn, increasingly unwilling to participate in the social scene, and it caused an inevitable rift in our relationship. An irreversible one, I considered,' she explained with a certain degree of helplessness. 'Especially when it seemed to be compounded by your all too frequent business trips.'

She stood hesitant and silent, her eyes unconsciously begging him to say something—*anything*.

CHAPTER NINE

'EVEN now, you really don't know, do you?' Raf queried with deceptive quietness.

Chelsea swallowed nervously, unsure and terribly afraid that what he was about to say might alter the pattern of her life. Had he tired of her already? Decided he had to return to the States? Maybe he wanted a divorce . . . *No!* Something deep inside her screamed in silent agony, and she lowered her gaze in self-defence as she willed her voice to remain steady. 'I was never very good at guessing games.'

He was silent for a few lengthy seconds, and she held her breath, waiting for him to continue.

'The mystery buyer was an elaborate invention used specifically to provide me with a reason to be in Australia,' he told her silkily, and it took a tremendous effort for her to force any words through the sudden constriction in her throat.

'I see.'

'Do you, Chelsea?' His lips twisted into a cynical smile, and the tiny flutter that had begun in the region of her heart gained an unsteady momentum.

'I can't imagine you lacking the initiative to go after whatever you wanted,' she said shakily and her eyes flew open as Raf lifted her chin to meet his gaze.

'Sam knew that healthwise he was on borrowed time,' he revealed with unaccustomed gentleness.

'He had no son to whom he could bequeath his empire, only a beautiful daughter he feared would be the mark of numerous fortune-hunters once he died.' His eyes kindled with something she was unable to define. 'Through extreme anxiety he did the unforgivable and deliberately sought suitable husband material, baiting the figurative hook with the promise of a merger in the Houghton firm, painstakingly searching until he found the right company with the right man at its head. Hamilton met all his requirements.' His voice became cynical, his smile a mere facsimile. 'I was tired of the social circuit, its predictability. Paula had become an increasing problem from which I continually sought escape, and the presence of a wife would provide a protective bond. Sam's proposition, together with your photograph, was sufficiently persuasive,. and I agreed to meet you.' He paused, then dug his hands deep into his trouser pockets and looked at her, his eyes warm and incredibly gentle.

'You were extremely beautiful, entertainingly witty, and I deliberately fostered the attraction, aware within days that having you as my wife would be no hardship at all.'

Chelsea felt her eyes widen, then begin to ache with unshed tears at he lifted a hand and traced the outline of her mouth.

'Of all the lovers I'd ever known, you were the most generous, unspoilt——' He broke off, offering her a crooked smile as he caressed her cheek. 'Special.'

She was powerless to utter so much as a word and her lips trembled beneath his touch.

'If you were unsure of me before Sam's death, you were doubly vulnerable afterwards.' Raf's eyes bored into hers, dark, unfathomable, and a tiny muscle clenched at the edge of his jaw as he attempted some form of control. 'I wanted to fly out to Australia and physically drag you back to the States when you refused to rejoin me, but such an action would have achieved nothing—expect perhaps to have you condemn me for being an arrogant, insensitive husband.'

There wasn't a single thing Chelsea could think of to say, and she stood speechless, almost too frightened to breathe in case she broke the intangible spell binding them close to ultimate understanding.

'You needed time and some space of your own for a while.' Pain clouded his expression for a brief second before it was successfully masked. 'You had a degree in business management, which, given a fraction of Sam's inherited genes, deserved an opportunity to be put into practice. I hoped that after a few months you might begin to miss me, to want and need me as much as I needed you. I picked up the phone nearly every day, replaced the receiver before the call could connect. As difficult as it was for *me*, I knew there was nothing to be gained from forcing a confrontation too soon. So I installed Jonathan, primarily to keep me informed of your progress. Twice in the last year I flew in to Sydney with the intention of seeing you, only to board an outward bound jet within days of arrival.'

He had been in Sydney, *twice*, and she hadn't known? It seemed too incredible to contemplate.

'The global share-market fiasco was providential

in that it enabled me to concoct a logical reason for my presence here without unduly arousing your suspicions.' Raf paused fractionally, then ventured quietly, 'I imagined arranging a reconciliation would be easy.'

She had been so willing to discredit his every move, she had ignored the obvious and conducted a senseless war with her own emotions.

'There's something I want you to have,' Raf declared, and his eyes never left her face as he moved a few paces to her mother's writing-desk. Reaching out, he opened the top, then extracted a long, slim envelope from an inside drawer and handed it to her.

Chelsea looked at him for what seemed an age, then she slowly took the envelope between nerveless fingers. She ran the tip of her forefinger along its creased edge, oddly reluctant to break the seal.

'Open it.'

Inside was a folded paper, a letter, she discovered, with the heading of a highly reputable American banking insitution. Addressed to her, it revealed a total of funds held to her credit in a specified account relating to deposits made by Rafael Hamilton over a period of three years.

'I signed the shares I originally bought in Houghton over to you a month after our marriage,' Raf told her. 'Those funds represent dividends and my directorial fee as head as the Houghton-Hamilton board.'

There were so many questions demanding an answer, Chelsea hardly knew where to begin. 'Why?' The single query slipped out before she could retract it.

Raf lifted a hand to her hair, threading his fingers

through its length in a oddly caressing gesture. 'I wanted you to have tangible proof of how I felt. *Love*. The heights and depths, the agony and ecstasy of an emotion I'd grown weary of believing I would ever experience.'

Chelsea felt her heart tilt, then begin an accelerated beat as warmth flooded through her veins, filling her body with a delicious glow. All she could do was look at him in speechless fascination.

'Those so-called bedmates you refer to were nothing more than that—decorative companions who were convenient partners to various functions. Eager for an entrée into the homes of the rich and famous,' Raf explained with a trace of cynicism. 'And there were not that many, and none after you.'

For a moment she stood frozen, her brain refusing to assimilate his meaning. *None*? He'd remained celibate for two years? But then, hadn't *she*?

'How could I?' Raf queried gently. 'When the only woman I wanted was *you*. To be embraced, encased within your sweet body, part of you.'

'I think,' Chelsea said shakily, 'I need to sit down.'

Raf's husky laugh echoed softly in her ears. 'I had something more comfortable in mind, such as a bed. Somewhere I can pleasure you with my body, show you as no words can that I love you. So much,' he added gently, a faint smile teasing his lips at the joy he saw reflected in her eyes. 'Perhaps I'd better demonstrate,' he drawled musingly, pulling her inextricably close as he lowered his head to hers.

She opened her mouth the instant his lips met hers wanting to savour the eroticism only he could offer. Of their own volition her hands crept up to entwine themselves at his nape, and her body moved subtly closer to his, exulting in its arousal.

She barely heard his faintly audible groan, then his mouth hardened, slaking a passionate thirst that matched her own, and it seemed an eternity before his lips gentled; brushing, tasting the slight grazing of the delicate inner tissue before teasing the fullness of her mouth with the tip of his tongue.

From there he trailed a path down the vulnerable, pulsing cord at the edge of her neck, and buried his mouth in the gentle hollow, his touch an exquisite torture as he caressed the delicate indentations along the base of her throat before seeking the lobe of her ear, taking it between his teeth and biting the sensitive flesh with just sufficient pressure to send a tremor raking through her body.

Without a word he curved an arm beneath her knees and lifted her high against his chest to carry her through to the bedroom.

There he let her slide down to her feet, then gently, with infinite care, he slowly slid the straps of her maillot down over her shoulders, easing the thin slither of satiny stretch-silk from her breasts until it slipped down into a small heap on the carpet at her feet. His eyes were dark, launguorous, as they encompassed her slim curves, and she felt her breasts grow heavy beneath his gaze, their rose peaks burgeoning in anticipation of the sweet torture his tormenting mouth would provide.

In unison, the slow ache deep within began to radiate, inflaming her with a desire so potent that she trembled, wanting, *needing* him so much that it was impossible to deny being apart from him any longer.

Raf lifted a hand and trailed his fingers across her

lips, and she marvelled at the faint tremor in their touch.

Without thought she caught hold of his hand and held it against her mouth, parting it to gently kiss each finger in turn; then she reached for the band of his swimming trunks, her own fingers shaky as they slid the garment off his hips, her eyes wide, expressive pools as Raf added his assistance until he too stood unadorned, his skin gleaming, glistening with the faint sexual heat emanating from his taut frame.

'Beautiful,' he muttered huskily as his fingers traced a path down the column of her throat to the swollen peak of her breast, caressing it gently with his thumb before sliding to cup its entire fullness within his hand. Not content, he explored her ribcage, the tender curve of her waist, trailing inwardly to tease the concave indentation of her navel, the soft slightness of her stomach, before moving lower to seek the central core of her being.

It was almost more than she could bear, and she took the final step that brought her into his arms, exulting in the feel of his skin against her own as she wrapped her arms around his waist and held him close; wordless, her cheeks buried against the mat of chest hair, needing these few moments to absorb the fact that he really loved her.

Then slowly she raised her head and lifted her hands to capture his face, pulling it down to hers as she initiated a kiss that left him in no doubt of her feelings. Her heart was in her eyes, in the touch of her lips as it roamed the harsh contours of his face.

'I never stopped loving you,' she whispered, feeling her whole body vibrate as it reacted to the gentle stroking action of his hands as they caressed her skin, exploring with a tactile, sensual sureness that brought alive every pleasure pulse and unleashed a primitive, erotic abandon.

'You caused me a number of sleepless nights wondering if you had,' Raf confessed with a certain wryness. 'The past two years have been the worst in my life!'

'And mine. I desperately wanted to recapture those first few months we had together,' Chelsea declared quietly. 'The sheer feeling we were able to share, the loving. It all seemed part of an incredible dream which gradually began to go horribly wrong.'

Raf lifted his hands to capture her shoulders. 'I can promise that no one, ever, will come close enough to sow any seeds of uncertainty, or cast any more doubts. And immediately after the New Year we're flying to the Greek Islands for an extended second honeymoon.' He smiled faintly, almost with philosophical self-derision. 'Look at me, Chelsea. See the effect you have.'

His voice trembled slightly, and her eyes widened with incredulity that the man who commanded such an enormous corporation, whose power had become legendary, could be reduced to any degree of vulnerability.

'You touch my hand in the night, and I wake up shaking, afraid for a moment that your presence in my bed is merely a fragment of another tormented dream.'

Unbidden, her tongue parted her mouth and its tip edged slowly along her lower lip. How could she have been so blind? Choosing her words with care, she extended her hand and felt his warm clasp. 'Let's go back to bed.' She searched his beloved face and saw his eyes darken with undisguised passion.

A soft bubble of laughter emerged from her throat as confidence gave her the impetus to tease him a little. 'Although of course we *should* consider a shower, then dress for breakfast and drive to the office. Do you want to?' she queried wickedly, tilting her head to one side in apparent consideration. 'I think I can conjure up sufficient enthusiasm, if you can. But of course, if you'd rather not . . .' She let her voice trail off as Raf lifted a hand and pressed his fingers against her lips, tilting her chin fractionally with his thumb.

'Fool,' he smiled softly. 'The office can do without us.' His features gentled, and what she saw revealed there made her ache so much, she wanted to cry.

Without a word she gently pulled him down on to the mattress before sitting up to kneel beside him. 'This is for you,' she said shakily, unsure if she had quite the measure of courage necessary to initiate what she intended. 'With all my love.'

As if he guessed her faint reserve, Raf lifted a hand to her cheek and smiled. 'Don't be shy. I would adore for you to pleasure me in any way you choose.'

And she did, beginning with the strong column of his throat, her mouth warm and caressing as it conducted a slow, seductive, exploratory path over every inch of his body, until his ragged breathing and increasing loss of control brought forth a despairing groan that begged release. She gave it, guiding him inside her, exultant as he captured the tender peak of her breast and teased it unmercifully with his tongue until it was her turn to cry out against the shaft of sensation that shuddered its way through her body. Wave after wave, until she thought it would never ease, then he gently rolled her on to her back and proceeded to reciprocate with such infinite dedication that she became a total wanton beneath his skilled touch, wild with abandon as she pleaded for his possession.

It was a long time before he released her, and she lay spent in his arms, her legs entwined with his, her cheek resting against his chest.

'Where shall we live?' she murmured after a while, too sated with love to conduct much of a conversation, yet curious to learn his plans for their future.

Raf's lips lifted from their drifting exploration of the hollows at the edge of her temple. 'Wherever you want,' he murmured huskily, and she felt a faint bubble of amusement rise to the surface.

'Really?'

'Yes. Does that make you feel giddy with the power you have over me?'

For a moment Chelsea went still, aware that he was merely teasing, but in a way she found it vaguely frightening. 'I'm not sure I want you to bow down to my every want and need.' She tried to make it light, and didn't quite succeed.

He raised his head, glimpsed her faint indecision, and laughed. 'No?' I fully intend to cherish you, *querida*, and treasure all the days and nights we spend together.' Dark eyes gleamed with genuine amusement. 'Especially the nights!'

She felt her pulse trip and begin a faster beat.

'Idiot,' she chastised weakly. 'Be serious!'

'I am—perfectly serious. As to where we'll live—it doesn't matter. With the advantages of modern technology I can be instantly aware of any developments anywhere in the world. Available to make a decision at the flick of an electronic button.'

It was nothing less than the truth. Slowly Chelsea reached up a hand to trace her fingers down the lean strong length of his jaw. 'Perhaps,' she ventured, 'we could alternate between Australia and America. Your parents are entitled to see you more than once or twice a year, and when we have children I'd like them to know their grandparents and enjoy the pleasure of aunts and uncles and cousins. Family,' she added with unintentional wistfulness.

Raf shifted slightly, leaning forward as he rested a hand either side of her face. 'I like the sound of that.'

'Would you mind very much if I was selfish and said I'd like some time alone with you first? A special year just for us?' There was nothing in his expression to tell her whether he approved or not, and she rushed into breathless explanation. 'I'll only be twenty-six——'

She broke off as his mouth closed unerringly over hers, possessing its inner sweetness with such bewitching sensuality that she felt herself drawn into a vortex of swirling emotion.

It seemed an age before he relinquished her lips, and by then she was spellbound, held mesmerised within a web of passion where nothing else mattered.

'You're beautiful, do you know that?' Raf said gently. 'Everything I could possibly want, all I'll ever need.' His lips sought and found the delicate whorls

of her ear, teasing the intricate orifice with the tip of
his tongue before slipping across to press his mouth
against her closed eyes.

'Will you let me retain a working interest in
Houghton-Hamimlton?' The words left her lips
before she'd given them too much thought. Yet she
felt alive meeting the challenge of being involved in
the business world, and, while she recognised that
raising children and being Raf's social hostess would
occupy a very important part in her life, she had no
wish to remain idly at home until such time as she
became pregnant.

'On one condition,' Raf murmured against her
throat as his lips trailed to the pulse at its base, feeling
its quickened beat as his fingers brushed lightly
across the contours of her breast. 'You accompany
me wherever I happen to travel in the world.' He
kissed her gently, savouring the feel of her mouth,
and the joyous unreserved response to his touch. 'I
want you with me. By my side—always.'

Chelsea's eyes acquired a deep, lustrous gleam,
and her lips became faintly tremulous as they parted
to form a deliciously curved smile. 'Thank you,' she
said simply. 'For caring, believing in me.'

'I always have,' he assured her with unaccustomed
gravity, and she felt a warm, relaxed sensation flood
her body, a sense of complete peace.

Everything he said was true, except that she had
been too easily swayed in the beginning to realise it,
too inexperienced to trust in him, in herself. Almost
as if she'd touched the flame of love and been
burned; unwilling to become involved again for fear
of being hurt.

Now there were no doubts, no illusion. Just love. Consuming, inviolate—unashamedly theirs.

Harlequin Presents

Coming Next Month

1247 KING OF THE MOUNTAIN Melinda Cross
Ross Arnett is a superb fashion photographer He's also a good man in emergencies, as Marnie discovers when she has to follow him down a mountain in a blizzard.

1248 A SECURE MARRIAGE Diana Hamilton
Cleo proposes to her dynamic boss, Jude Mescal—not out of love, but in desperation. His surprising acceptance solves one of her problems but creates another. For what can Jude possibly gain from their marriage?

1249 TUSCAN ENCOUNTER Madeleine Ker
Claudia buys the perfect farmhouse for herself and Vito, her fiancé, only to have the ownership disputed by the powerful Cesare di Stefano. The battle looms long and bitter until, among the verbal sparring, sparks of attraction start to fly.

1250 NIGHT WITH A STRANGER Joanna Mansell
It's out of character for Lorel to blow a lot of money on a holiday. But not as out of character as her behavior when she finds herself sitting beside Lewis Elliott on the Orient Express to Venice!

1251 A FEVER IN THE BLOOD Anne Mather
Cassandra flees to Italy and to Ben—the only person who can help her Then she realizes she's adding to her problems, not solving them, when the old attraction between them flares up again.

1252 THE LOVE CONSPIRACY Susan Napier
Kate feels like a misfit in the life-style of her friend Todd's family, but resents their superior air. She decides to teach them a lesson, especially Todd's uncle, Daniel Bishop—not knowing that she is the pawn in quite another game.

1253 WILD ENCHANTMENT Kate Proctor
Jilly would never have told Jean-Luc de Sauvignet about her injury if she'd known that his doctorate wasn't in medicine. But she had, and now it seems that with very little effort he can ruin her career—and happiness.

1254 FRIDAY'S CHILD Stephanie Wyatt
Mirry has misgivings about how Jay Elphick will fit into village life once he inherits Wenlow Hall—but she is prepared to welcome him. She has no idea, though, just how much he holds their family past against her

Available in March wherever paperback books are sold, or through Harlequin Reader Service:

In the U.S.
901 Fuhrmann Blvd.
P.O. Box 1397
Buffalo, N.Y 14240-1397

In Canada
P.O. Box 603
Fort Erie, Ontario
L2A 5X3

February brings you...

Harlequin Presents...

Award of Excellence

PENNY JORDAN

valentine's night

Sorrel didn't particularly want to meet her long-lost cousin Val from Australia. However, since the girl had come all this way just to make contact, it seemed a little churlish not to welcome her.

As there was no room at home, it was agreed that Sorrel and Val would share the Welsh farmhouse that was being renovated for Sorrel's brother and his wife. Conditions were a bit primitive, but that didn't matter.

At least, not until Sorrel found herself snowed in with the long-lost cousin, who turned out to be a handsome, six-foot male!

Also, look for the next Harlequin Presents Award of Excellence title in April:

Elusive as the Unicorn
by Carole Mortimer

HP1243-1

You'll flip . . . your pages won't!
Read paperbacks *hands-free* with

Book Mate • I

The perfect "mate" for all your romance paperbacks

**Traveling • Vacationing • At Work • In Bed • Studying
• Cooking • Eating**

Perfect size for all standard paperbacks, this wonderful invention makes reading a pure pleasure! Ingenious design holds paperback books OPEN and FLAT so even wind can't ruffle pages— leaves your hands free to do other things. Reinforced, wipe-clean vinyl-covered holder flexes to let you turn pages without undoing the strap . . . supports paperbacks so well, they have the strength of hardcovers!

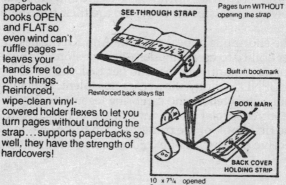

Pages turn WITHOUT opening the strap

SEE-THROUGH STRAP

Reinforced back stays flat

Built in bookmark

BOOK MARK

BACK COVER HOLDING STRIP

10 x 7¼ opened
Snaps closed for easy carrying, too

Available now. Send your name, address, and zip code, along with a check or money order for just $5.95 + .75¢ for postage & handling (for a total of $6.70) payable to Reader Service to:

Reader Service
Bookmate Offer
901 Fuhrmann Blvd.
P.O. Box 1396
Buffalo, N.Y. 14269-1396

Offer not available in Canada
*New York and Iowa residents add appropriate sales tax.

BM-G

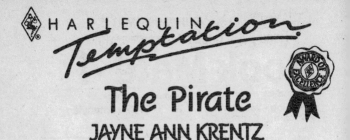

The Pirate
JAYNE ANN KRENTZ

At the heart of every powerful romance story lies a legend. There are many romantic legends and countless modern variations on them, but they all have one thing in common: They are tales of brave, resourceful women who must gentle and tame the powerful, passionate men who are their true mates.

The enormous appeal of Jayne Ann Krentz lies in her ability to create modern-day versions of these classic romantic myths, and her LADIES AND LEGENDS trilogy showcases this talent. Believing that a storyteller who can bring legends to life deserves special attention, Harlequin has chosen the first book of the trilogy—THE PIRATE—to receive our Award of Excellence. Look for it now.

AE-PIR-1A